W9-BXE-387

TREMENDOUS THINGS

ALSO BY SUSIN NIELSEN

No Fixed Address

Optimists Die First

We Are All Made of Molecules

The Reluctant Journal of Henry K. Larsen

Dear George Clooney: Please Marry My Mom

Word Nerd

TREMENDOUS THINGS

A Novel

SUSIN NIELSEN

WENDY

Text copyright © 2021 by Susin Nielsen
Jacket art used under license from Shutterstock.com

All rights reserved. Published in the United States by Wendy Lamb Books, an imprint of Random House Children's Books, a division of Penguin Random House LLC, New York.

Wendy Lamb Books and the colophon are trademarks of Penguin Random House LLC.

Visit us on the Web! rhcbooks.com

Educators and librarians, for a variety of teaching tools, visit us at RHTeachersLibrarians.com

Library of Congress Cataloging-in-Publication Data
Names: Nielsen-Fernlund, author.
Title: Tremendous things / Susin Nielsen.
Description: [New York] : Wendy Lamb Books, [2021] | Audience: Ages 12 and up. | Audience: Grades 7–9. | Summary: Branded by a middle school humiliation, fourteen-year-old Wilbur needs help from friends Alex, Fabrizio, and elderly neighbor Sal to impress Charlie, a French girl whose school band is doing an exchange with his.
Identifiers: LCCN 2020020739 (print) | LCCN 2020020740 (ebook) |
ISBN 978-1-5247-6838-6 (hardcover) | ISBN 978-1-5247-6839-3 (library binding) |
ISBN 978-1-5247-6841-6 (trade paperback) | ISBN 978-1-5247-6840-9 (ebook)
Subjects: CYAC: Popularity—Fiction. | High schools—Fiction. | Schools—Fiction. | Foreign study—Fiction. | Bands (Music)—Fiction. | Lesbian mothers—Fiction.
Classification: LCC PZ7.N565 Tre 2021 (print) | LCC PZ7.N565 (ebook) | DDC [Fic]—dc23

The text of this book is set in 11-point Adobe Text Pro.
Interior design by Cathy Bobak

Printed in the United States of America
10 9 8 7 6 5 4 3 2 1
First Edition

To every one of you who march to your own beat:
you are terrific. Radiant. Some human being!

THEN

THE MUMPS BELIEVE THAT WE ALL HAVE A HANDFUL OF Defining Moments in our lives.

Their Number One Defining Moment was the night they met each other, sixteen years ago, at a screening of *The Rocky Horror Picture Show* in Vancouver. Dr. Frank-N-Furter had just declared, "A toast!" Mum threw her piece of toast at the screen and hit Mup in the back of the head. The rest, as they say, is history. They've been madly in love ever since. It has a happy ending, which I think we can all agree is the best kind of story.

My Number One Defining Moment doesn't have a happy ending.

In fact, it hasn't even ended.

The moment in question happened two and a half years ago, on my first day of seventh grade. We'd recently moved to Toronto, so it was also a brand-new school.

Oh, and it was also my first school ever.

Aside from a disastrous few weeks in kindergarten, I'd been homeschooled my whole life. But when we moved from Vancouver to Toronto, we made a family decision: it was time for me to get educated, and socialized, in an actual brick-and-mortar building filled with actual flesh-and-blood kids.

Mum and Mup—collectively known as the Mumps—walked me to Pierre Elliott Trudeau Junior School that first morning in September. They hugged and kissed me and cried a little right out front as all the other kids streamed past, which now that I think about it probably wasn't the best optics.

What I remember most about entering that massive old red-brick building for the first time was the noise. I'd been around other kids before, obviously; I'd had frequent outings and get-togethers with other homeschooled kids. But we're talking ten to fifteen kids at a time, tops. The halls of PET Junior School were packed, with *hundreds* of kids shouting, laughing, banging locker doors, running even though there were signs telling them to walk. My first instinct was to turn around and march right back out. But I thought of what Mup had said the night before, when I couldn't sleep: "Remember, Wil: new beginnings bring new experiences."

So I kept moving.

My pits were dripping with fear-sweat by the time I found my classroom. Our teacher, Mr. Markowitz, stood by his desk. I can still picture him in his brown suit, the shoulders dusted with dandruff. He gave us an assignment. "Write a letter to yourself. Describe who you are today. Then write a list of goals you hope

4

to achieve by the time you graduate high school. Place your letter in the envelope provided, write your name on the front, and seal it. The letters will be locked into the school's time capsule. And remember," he continued, "you can be completely honest. These letters are for your eyes only. They will be returned to you, still sealed, six years from now, on graduation day."

I was determined to do exactly as I was told.

So I was completely honest.

After school, Mr. Markowitz carried the sealed letters from our classroom to the time capsule, which wasn't really a time capsule at all but the safe in the principal's office. It was a short walk from our homeroom, down a flight of stairs and to the left.

But at the top of the staircase, according to a reliable eyewitness, Mr. Markowitz stopped to scratch his balls.

This had a ring of truth to it, because as we learned that year, Mr. Markowitz scratched his balls a lot. He did it so much, a rumor spread that he had pubic lice.

While he scratched, one letter fluttered, unseen, to the ground.

Mine.

Time Capsule Letter, Graduating Class of 2025

Name: Wilbur Alberto Nuñez-Knopf

Age: 11 and ¾

Describe Yourself As You Are Today: I am five feet four inches tall. Farah, one of my homeschool friends in Vancouver, told me I could play a young Marty

Feldman if they ever made a biopic about him, which I thought was a compliment until we watched *Young Frankenstein.* Farah also nicknamed me "Blubber" because (a) I'm chubby, and (b) I cry a lot. The Mumps keep saying that (a) it's baby fat and I'll have a growth spurt soon, and (b) there is no shame in crying and the world needs more sensitive men. They also keep saying I'll grow into my looks. I hope they're right.

I also hope that if I grow taller, Jeremiah grows with me, because right now he's the size of a tadpole. And I hope I can learn to control him better, because recently he's started popping up at embarrassing moments for no reason. Like right now. I've had to put a textbook over my lap.

What else can I say about me? I want to be a writer when I grow up. I write a lot!! Mostly short stories about dinosaurs and outer space. Boy, I can get really lost in my make-believe worlds, which is good because we just moved to Toronto a month ago and I have a total of zero friends! I'm dying to get a pet, but the Mumps say I have to wait. I had a cat named Snickerdoodle in Vancouver, but he didn't come home one day. The Mumps said he probably found another family.

Farah said he probably got eaten by a coyote.

Goals You Would Like to Achieve by the Time You Graduate:

1) Grow taller.

2) Grow Jeremiah.

3) Learn to control Jeremiah.

4) Cry less! It may be good for men to show their feelings, but if I cry one more time at that SPCA ad with Sarah McLachlan singing I will punch myself in the face—just thinking of it right now is making me tear up.

5) Make friends! I didn't have a ton of friends in Vancouver except for Stewart Inkster, and once in a while another homeschooler like Farah. The Mumps keep saying *they* are my friends, but they are also my mothers, so I'm not sure they count.

6) Publish some of my writing! I know this is a long shot before the end of high school, and I also know every artist has to suffer some rejection, but as Mup says, "every dream begins with a dreamer."

7) Have a Loving and Mutually Respectful Relationship (Mumps™) with a special girl. Fall in love! (And maybe, *just maybe,* once we are deeply in

love, I could feel one of her boobs. Or both. But only with her Enthusiastic Consent (Mumps™)!

8) Last but definitely not least: Learn to be my best self. Try not to be so timid and nervous all the time. Be more willing and able to try new things. Put myself out there. Be confident and brave.

Like Mup says: "He who takes no chances wins nothing!"

Signed,
Wilbur Alberto Nuñez-Knopf

AT FIRST I THOUGHT I WAS IMAGINING THINGS WHEN I showed up at school the next day. Surely every single kid wasn't *actually* staring at me.

I was not imagining things.

Someone had opened my letter—*my personal, private letter*—and taken photos of it. Then that person had posted it on every social media platform known to personkind, where it had been liked by and shared with every single kid at my new school and beyond.

By ten a.m. I was hiding in the nurse's office, crying worse than I ever had during the SPCA ad.

By eleven a.m. the Mumps had been called in for an emergency meeting. I guess the principal decided I couldn't be more humiliated than I already was, because she let them read my letter off *her* phone. She assured them that the school would find the guilty party and they would be dealt with.

On the drive home I was still crying a lot, so Mum sat in the back with me and held my hand. She'd come straight from the set of *Where There's a Wolf,* and she was in full special effects makeup; her hand was hairy. "This isn't the end of the world, peanut. It may feel like it right now, but you will rise above it."

"Mum's right," Mup replied, peering at me through the rearview mirror of our new Hyundai. "What doesn't kill you makes you stronger."

I let out a sob. Mum pulled me toward her, and I felt her hairy cheeks. "For what it's worth, I thought it was a lovely letter. Honest and to the point."

"And trust us, there is not a boy in your class who hasn't suffered the indignities of a spontaneous erection," Mup added from the front as I slouched even lower in my seat.

Mum stroked my hair. "We do have one tiny bone to pick with you, peanut."

Oh, no.

"Did you really have to use the word *boobs*? We've been so careful to teach you the anatomically correct names for body parts."

"Ditto *Jeremiah.* It was cute when you were young, but I'm not sure it's still age-appropriate or healthy to be anthropomorphizing your penis." Mup sighed. "I blame myself for playing 'Joy to the World' a lot when you were little."

It was true that I'd lifted the name from the song, because

Jeremiah looked like a bullfrog. And he was a good friend of mine.

"To be clear, Wil: you want to feel a girl's *breasts*," said Mum. "And you want a bigger *penis*." She smiled, revealing sharp, pointy werewolf teeth.

In case it isn't obvious, I am an only child.

The Mumps did their best to stay upbeat that evening. They even pulled out the karaoke machine and tried to nudge me into singing "I Will Survive" by Gloria Gaynor. (I refused.)

Later that night, though, I made a trip to the bathroom to pee, and I overheard them talking in their bedroom.

Mum: "I knew that school was a bad idea."

Mup: "Norah, come on. How could you possibly know?"

Mum: "For the same reasons we chose to homeschool him, Carmen. One, he's a preemie. Two, he's a December baby. And three—well, he's not exactly socially adept, is he? Remember kindergarten? He cried every single day for three weeks until we finally pulled him out."

Mup: "And maybe, if we'd left him in for a fourth week, he'd have stopped crying and started fitting in."

Even though I couldn't see them, I could feel the icy chill in Mum's silence.

Mum: "I just want to do what's best for our boy. And that school isn't it."

Mup: "Darling Norah. I think we can both agree that our boy needs to learn how to navigate this big, crazy world we live in. Besides, what are our options? We can't homeschool him, not with your new gig and my work schedule."

Mum: "We could look into private school."

Mup: "And how on earth would we pay for it?"

Silence. Then:

Mum: "My heart breaks for him."

Mup: "I know. Mine does, too. But let's give it a few days. I'm sure they'll find the person responsible, and when they do—"

Mum: "We can string them up by their feet and pluck out their eyeballs with a spoon, then slowly disembowel them with a rusty old knife—"

Mup: "Ooh, you are such a Mama Bear." Then it grew silent again but this time I was pretty sure they were kissing. So I went back to bed and I tried to push all the bad thoughts out of my brain. I imagined instead that I was in the barn with the other animals in *Charlotte's Web,* because it was my favorite story of all time, and after a while it worked, and I fell asleep.

The school found the culprit almost immediately. Poppy, a girl in my grade, told the principal that after Mr. Markowitz dropped the letter, she'd seen Tyler Kertz pick it up.

I'd had exactly one interaction with Tyler, when I'd sat beside him in homeroom. "Nice hat," he'd said.

"Thanks. It's a Tilley original." Then: "I'm Wilbur Nuñez-Knopf." I held out my hand.

He didn't take it. "Do you have a condition or something?"

"What?"

"Your eyes. They bulge."

"N-n-no. They're just my eyes—"

"You look like a frog. Or a pug."

Then Mr. Markowitz entered, and that was that.

In spite of that—or maybe *because* of it?—when Tyler saw my name on the envelope, he didn't simply hand it back to Mr. Markowitz. He opened it, read it—then decided everyone else should read it, too.

When he was asked to explain himself, he told the principal that he'd done it "for a laugh." He hadn't meant any harm.

Kertz got a week's suspension, and he had to write me a letter of apology.

Me?

I was sentenced to an eternity in hell.

Helpless. My life in free fall . . .
My inner thoughts revealed to all

From "No Parachute" by Wilbur Nuñez-Knopf

"TIME HEALS ALL WOUNDS," MUP LIKES TO SAY. "AND TIME wounds all heels." I love Mup with all my heart. But some of her platitudes are a total crock.

After Tyler Kertz was suspended, we had one of our Family Dialogues. "We think you should try to stick it out for a bit," Mup said. "Running away from your problems is a race you'll never win." Mum emitted a strangled sound, and Mup took her hand and gripped it, hard. I was pretty sure they had a difference of opinion but had agreed to present a united front.

"Just one month, pickle," Mum said. "If things don't get better after that, we'll get you out." She made it sound like a jailbreak.

So I kept going to Pierre Elliott Trudeau Junior School.

And it was a nightmare.

The cracks about Jeremiah were endless. Some kids tried to

get me to cry on purpose, and I'm ashamed to admit they sometimes succeeded. Worse, nobody called me Wilbur anymore. I had a new nickname. None of us—not me, not Mum or Mup—had ever noticed the acronym my initials made.

Wank.

I hated going to school. I made up my mind that when the month was up, I would tell the Mumps I wanted out.

Then, just before the end of September, we were buried in an avalanche of bad luck.

Mup came home from work one day looking shaken. "I was replaced by a robot." She worked full-time at a grocery store as a cashier. They'd recently installed a bunch of self-serve checkout kiosks; since Mup was last in, she was first out. A few days later, Mum's TV show—her first starring gig, the whole reason we'd moved to Toronto—went up in flames. *Where There's a Wolf* starred Jennica Valentine and my mum, Norah Knopf, as leaders of a pack of female werewolves. But just two weeks into shooting, the producer was arrested for something called money laundering, and production shut down.

The Mumps scrambled to get jobs, any jobs. I heard them talking late at night; they were terrified we might lose the house we'd recently bought in the heart of Kensington Market. "We counted our chickens before they hatched," said Mup.

They were Stressed with a capital *S*.

So when the time came to have our family dialogue about school, I just said, "It's fine. I'm good. School's good." And all the little muscles in their faces relaxed, and I knew it was a huge relief, having one less thing to worry about, namely *me*.

I kept telling myself it was only two years. Then I would go to high school, where I could start fresh.

But I was an idiot.

Because Pierre Elliott Trudeau Senior School is right next door to Pierre Elliott Trudeau Junior School.

Meaning Tyler—and Wank—moved right along with me.

"HEY, FRANK, IS THAT A HALF A PACK OF CERTS IN YOUR pocket, or is Jeremiah happy to see me?" Kertz shouted in the hall this morning, our first day back after Christmas break. *Frank* is a new variation of my nickname; as he helpfully explained to me, "it's a combination of *Wank* and *Freak.*" So clever.

"You're slower than a sloth, *Wan*—I mean, Wilbur! Do another lap," our gym teacher, Mr. Urquhart, said during gym, because, yes, even he has learned my unfortunate nickname.

"Seat's taken, Wank," said Poppy in English class; Poppy, who used to be nice to me until, as a welcome-to-Senior-School gift to me, Tyler had started a rumor that I liked to sniff girls' bicycle seats. I mean, *come on.* I have never, not once, sniffed a bicycle seat. Or *any* seat, come to think of it. But some of the girls took it seriously, and they've refused to sit near me ever since.

"Excuse me, Wank? Could I borrow a pencil?" Jo Lin asked

in math class. This one stung the most, because Jo Lin is genuinely kind, to me and to everyone. She wasn't trying to be mean; she just thinks it's my *actual name*.

Even though I'm fourteen, a letter that I wrote when I was eleven—*eleven!*—still follows me like a bad smell. It's like nothing has changed in all that time. Like *I* haven't changed.

But I *have* changed. I'm much taller, for one. The Mumps were right; I had a massive growth spurt. It happened so fast, they joked that they could hear my bones creaking as they expanded. I literally had growing pains. Now I'm over six feet tall. But my height isn't an advantage; I don't play basketball or other team sports, because I'm a total klutz and I tend to duck whenever any type of ball is thrown in my direction. Also, even though I grew taller, I'm still pudgy and soft. And my hair is a weird wiry texture; Tyler likes to tell me it looks like a mass of brown pubes.

And, well, short of plucking them from my sockets, there is nothing I can do about my bulgy eyes.

Jeremiah grew with me, proportionally speaking. No one would hire him to be in pornos or anything. But he's average, like the person he's attached to. And the random pop-ups are (mostly) a thing of the past.

As for the rest of my list, I'm proud to say that I can now watch that Sarah McLachlan SPCA ad without crying at *least* forty percent of the time. Better still, I have one excellent friend—two, if you count Templeton—and for a while Alex and I were friends, but I'm not so sure where we stand anymore.

I still write all the time, although now I write mostly poetry; stories about dinosaurs and outer space was kid stuff (although, confession, I still love dinosaurs, but seriously, who doesn't?). And, no, I haven't published anything yet. But I try to tell myself that my personal suffering will make me a better writer. Tortured artist and all that.

Regarding number seven, no surprise, this has been an Epic Fail. I will never have a Mutually Loving and Respectful Relationship (Mumps™) before I graduate. Kertz made sure of that. The girls at my school look at me with suspicion, wariness, or sympathy—sometimes a combination of all three.

And eight—trying to be my best self, be brave, *blah, blah, blah—as if.* My goals are much simpler now: just try to make it through each day. Head down, mouth shut. Don't attract any unnecessary attention. He who takes no chances may win nothing, but, *news flash,* maybe he won't lose anything, either! 'Cause I've already lost some pretty big-ticket items, like (a) my dignity, (b) my self-respect, and (c) any confidence I once possessed.

My only goal now: try to survive.

Who Am I?

When I look in the mirror, who do I see?
The person I think I am
Or the person they perceive me to be?
Which one is the truth?
Which one is a lie?
Am I Wilbur, or Wank? I want to break down
and cry
If a tree falls in the forest
Does it make a sound?
If you're labeled, do you become the label?
(I know—that's profound)
No girl will ever love me
As long as I'm Wank
I'm viewed as an outcast, or worse
A blank
One person is to blame
For the state of my pain
He knows who he is, but I won't name his name
I dream sometimes that I push my tormentor
Into the path of a soul-sucking Dementor
Then I push him in front of a steamroller, too
So all that is left is a big smear of goo.

BY WILBUR NUÑEZ-KNOPF

"TELL ME ABOUT YOUR FIRST WEEK BACK AT SCHOOL,"
Sal said to me on Saturday morning. We were at side-by-side
lockers in the change room at the Jewish Community Center,
getting naked. I did my best to avert my gaze because (a) it's
rude to stare and (b) Sal is "eighty-five years young," so he is
very, very wrinkly, and I mean all over.

"It was okay," I replied. "The Trudeau-Manias have been rehearsing a lot. Mr. P wants us to sound good for our guests." Our
bandleader, Mr. Papadopoulos, had gone to a school orchestra
conference over the summer, and he'd met a bandleader from
Paris. Rumor had it that they'd had loads of s-e-x, and they'd
hatched up an exchange trip so they could see each other again.
The French students would arrive on Monday. "We got the name
of our exchange students," I told him. "Mine is Charlie Bourget."

"*Charlie* doesn't sound very French."

"I know, right? I was expecting an *Yves,* or a *Jacques.*" I pulled on my red Speedo under the shield of a towel. I do not have a Speedo body; I would much prefer to wear baggy swim shorts; but Sal gave me the Speedo for my birthday, and who am I to insult my best friend?

He held on to my arm for balance and we headed out of the change room, walking at a slow but steady pace. Technically I wasn't supposed to be in this class, not for another fifty years, at least, but Sal needed my help in the change room, so an exception was made.

Mup was already on the pool deck, her black curls tucked under a swim cap, her strong frame packed into a navy blue one-piece. The rest of her students—all women, all well past the age of sixty—milled around her. This is one of her three part-time jobs, and I'm pretty sure it's her favorite.

When the ladies saw us, they broke into grins. "Our boys are here!" said Ruth Gimbel. Because we're the only men in the class, Sal and I are treated like rock stars. The ladies pinch my cheeks and muss my wiry hair and bring me home-baked treats, which is pretty awesome.

But if I'm the drummer in the band, Sal is the heartthrob lead singer. The ladies *love* him. At least four of them, including Ruth, flirt with him because they know he's a widower and also, he's just a spectacular human being.

Mup started up her music. "All right everyone, into the water!"

Sal and I hopped into the pool. For the next hour, I let myself go in a way I never did anywhere else. I flung my arms up and shimmied left to right and did the cancan with my legs underwater.

Aquacise for Seniors is definitely one of the highlights of my week.

Mup had to teach more classes, so when we were done, Sal and I slow-walked to the Royal Ontario Museum, just a couple of blocks away. (Sal gives me a student membership for Christmas every year, and I give him a senior membership for Hanukkah every year.) Sal peered into his canvas carry bag. "What loot did you get today?"

"Nanaimo bars and chocolate chip cookies from the twins," I said. "You?"

"Same. And also an entire chocolate babka loaf from Ruth."

"She *so* has the hots for you."

"I don't disagree. But it's too soon."

"Irma died three years ago." I'd never met Sal's wife; she'd passed away before we moved in, but I knew he still missed her a lot.

"Exactly. Too soon. Plus, if you want the truth, Ruth is a little handsy. She touched my *derrière* three times in the pool today."

"Whoa. Bold."

"My sentiments exactly."

We entered the museum and made a beeline for Fulton, our nickname for the enormous dinosaur skeleton that dominates the museum foyer. Our shared love of all things dinosaur was one of the things Sal and I bonded over when we first met. He loaned me some books, and I read him the stories I'd written about a friendly but shy T. rex named, rather unimaginatively, Tex.

Fulton is not a T. rex; he's a replica of a Futalognkosaurus that roamed South America. He is *huge.* His feet rest on two metal slabs that stand a few feet apart.

We stepped between the slabs and the two of us lay down on the ground, hands behind our heads. We gazed up at Fulton's bones. It's one of Sal's favorite things to do. "Imagine, these creatures roamed this very planet millions and millions of years ago. It's incredible. Our lives are a blip! Tremendous! But still a blip!" he likes to say. "What a marvel life is!" Sal is full of wisdom that way; having a best friend who is seventy-one years older than me is a gift.

"You manage to make any weekend plans with Alex?" he asked as we stared up at Fulton's massive rib cage.

"No. I tried, but . . . he had plans."

"The boyfriend?"

I nodded.

"Ah. That's too bad. People can go a little nutty when they're in the first throes of romance."

"It's okay. It just means I get to spend more time with you."

"You need friends your own age too, Wilbur. *I* have friends my own age."

"Sal. Wilbur." José, the regular Saturday security guard,

26

loomed over us. His muscles bulged under his uniform. "You know what I'm gonna say."

Sal and José said in unison: "You can't lie on the floor in here. You're a hazard to yourselves and others." José reached down, took Sal's outstretched hands, and pulled him to his feet. He handed Sal his fedora.

"I have a treat for you, José." Sal reached into his carry bag and handed José one of his bags of goodies.

José's eyes lit up. "Nanaimo bars. Thanks, Sal."

We took the subway and a streetcar back to Sal's place, which is right next door to ours, part of a series of narrow, attached brick homes in Kensington Market. Some have been painted eye-popping colors, like ours, which is mauve. Sal's is the original redbrick. The insides of our houses are mirror images layoutwise, but the similarities end there: my family's place is full of stuff Mum has found on Craigslist and at garage sales; Sal's place is full of antiques.

As per our tradition, he made us grilled cheese sandwiches with Strub's pickles for lunch. This was partly because we love grilled cheese and partly because Sal's been retired for years and lives on a tight budget; I happen to know he eats a lot of grilled cheese, ramen noodles, and dented tins of soup.

At twelve thirty, he walked me to the door. "Here, take some babka for the road." He handed me two thick slices in a baggie.

* * *

I bid Sal goodbye and walked down to Foot Long Subs on Queen Street West. Over the Christmas holidays the owner, Mr. Chernov, had promoted me from Submarine Sandwich Creation Engineer to Submarine Sandwich Creation Expert. It didn't come with a raise, but Mr. Chernov reminded me that it did come with more responsibility, so I guess that's fair. Since Mr. Chernov was hardly ever there—he managed three franchises—technically I was now the supervisor of the other employees, but I'm not sure they'd gotten the memo.

"Dmitry, it's your turn to clean the washrooms," I told him early in our shift. Dmitry is new to Foot Long, short and sinewy with spiky hair, around my age; he's also what I would call a *problem employee.*

He was texting on his phone, and he didn't answer.

"Dmitry. You know the bathrooms need checking and refreshing once every hour."

"Sorry, no can do, Dilbert," he said without looking up.

"Wilbur," I said. "Why not?"

"Health reasons. I have psoriafungalitis."

I looked at him blankly.

"Skin condition. I can't use strong cleaning products, or I break out in a super-gross rash."

I knew I couldn't make him do something he was medically unfit for—I'd read the eighty-page manual, obvs—so I cleaned the washrooms myself. I don't know if it's unique to Foot Long or if it's a universal phenomenon, but there are tons of people who either don't understand *how* to flush, or simply don't *bother* to flush.

When Dmitry went on break Mitzi sidled up to me. She's also around my age, one or two inches shorter than me, with a powerful build, long red hair, and tortoiseshell glasses. "You know he made that up."

"Psoriafungalitis? No, I'm pretty sure it's a real thing."

Mitzi whipped out her phone and punched in the word. She held it out for me to see. "Nope."

"Oh."

We stood listening to the Muzak for a few moments. She checked her reflection in the window. "God, who designed these uniforms? Pikachu?"

Our uniforms are hideous—one-piece banana-yellow zip-up outfits made from cheap polyester. I'm guessing they were made to match the cheap, yellow plastic tables and chairs that are bolted to the franchise's floor. "For what it's worth, you look pretty good in yours," I said. "Like Sigourney Weaver in *Alien*. Or Uma Thurman in *Kill Bill*."

"Meaning, kind of badass?"

"Definitely."

That got a rare smile; most of the time, Mitzi looks disdainful and bored. I have no idea what she thinks of me.

If I am totally honest, I find her rather terrifying.

* * *

Mitzi and I worked steadily during our shift, unlike Dmitry, who kept disappearing for long stretches into the back. He left fifteen minutes before his shift was officially over.

George and Deepak took over for Mitzi and me at six. Since it was after dark, I walked her home. "You really don't have to do this," she said. "I have a blue belt in karate. I could take down a guy twice your size, and way more handily than you ever could, no offense."

"None taken. And I believe you. But it's on my way."

She lives on Shaw Street, and since we were together we cut through Trinity-Bellwoods Park. "I think Franklin's sick," she told me. It took me a moment to remember that Franklin was her pet turtle. "He's slowing down."

"But . . . isn't that just being a turtle?"

"Trust me, I can tell. Franklin and I are pretty tight."

I dropped her in front of her house. "Well I hope he picks up his pace soon," I said. "And remember, I won't be at work for a week."

"Oh, right. Your exchange students. Hope it's fun." Mitzi did a pirouette, waved goodbye, and headed up her front walk.

She is a mystery wrapped in an enigma.

When I opened our front door, I was greeted by a blast of warm air, CBC Radio, and Templeton, who scampered into the foyer on his short little legs with a series of delighted, high-pitched barks. "Who's my good boy?" I said in a baby voice. "Who's my good sweet boy?" I scooped him into my arms. He aggressively licked my face.

We headed into the kitchen. Mup's legs stuck out from under the sink. She likes to say, "When the going gets tough, the tough get going." That's what she did after she was laid off. On top of her three part-time jobs, she decided that if we couldn't afford to hire anyone to fix our fixer-upper, she'd do it herself. She watches YouTube videos on everything from plastering to basic plumbing; she's completely self-taught. But she's also only one woman, and she lives with two spatially-and-mechanically-challenged individuals, so the fixing up is slow going.

I put Templeton down just as Mup crawled out from under the sink, a triumphant grin on her face. "Fixed the leak. I'll get dinner started— Ugh. Wil." Mup pointed at Templeton. He was pulling himself across the floor by his front legs, dragging his bum along the linoleum. "You know what that means."

I did. "Do I have to do it right now?"

"He's leaving skid marks of poo on the floor. And you know what we agreed on. You're his—"

"Primary caregiver. I know." This had been made clear to me when the Mumps let me adopt him. I scooped him up again, holding him a little farther away this time. "You're lucky I love you so much," I whispered into his good ear. Then I carried him upstairs to do the deed.

Once we were done, I took Templeton to our local parkette for a quick pre-dinner walk. The walls on two sides are covered in colorful murals and graffiti. Lloyd, who runs the Jamaican patty shop, and Viktor, who runs the cheese shop, sat on their favorite bench in their parkas, smoking a joint. They're fixtures in the park, no matter the weather or the time of day. We said our hellos. Lloyd added, "That is a face only a mother could love." I wasn't sure if he was talking about Templeton or me.

When we got back, Mum was in the kitchen too, setting the table. She was dressed in a business suit, her long, dark hair piled on top of her head. My mothers are both beautiful women: Carmen is short and Rubenesque, with masses of black curls; Norah is tall and slender, with long, chestnut hair and incredible cheekbones. I only mention this because how Mum gave birth to a troll like me is a mystery. Especially since the donor's profile page said he was *a handsome Harvard grad who almost made the Olympic rowing team. . . .*

I think he was more likely *a very good liar who donated his sperm because he needed the extra cash.*

Mup put bowls of kale-and-white-bean soup on our small Formica table. She cooks on the days she gets home first, and those are the best days because she is a much better cook than Mum, but we keep this to ourselves because Mum gets defensive if we mention it.

We took turns telling each other about our days. It's a Nuñez-Knopf family tradition. When it was Mum's turn she said, "I was background in a restaurant scene today. I had to pretend to be in love with this old fart. He must have been thirty years my senior. It was dull as dishwater." After *Where There's a Wolf* went up in flames, Mum's acting career followed suit. But, like Carmen, Norah is resourceful. She decided that no role was too small, and now she takes on a lot of work as a background performer. She also has a great eye for finding vintage items at garage sales; she cleans them up or refurbishes them, then sells them for a profit on Etsy.

I slurped up the last of my soup. "I don't think I mentioned," I said, knowing full well I hadn't, "Mr. Papadopoulos needs the deposit for the exchange trip by Friday." The French students weren't just coming to stay with us; we were supposed to visit them in Paris, too, in April. I guess that's why it's called an *exchange*. The school Parent Action Committee was covering some of the costs, but we were responsible for most of it.

The Mumps exchanged a glance. "How much?"

"Four hundred dollars," I said. "The total is sixteen hundred."

I heard a stereo sucking in of breath. Mum busied herself with taking down one of the many retro cookie jars that line the tops of the cupboards.

"I've been giving it a lot of thought," I said. "I don't have to go to Paris. I don't think I'd enjoy it, anyway."

"Why on earth not?" asked Mup.

"Different language, different foods, different culture . . ." I made a face.

"It's true you don't like change," said Mum. She took some of her homemade pumpkin cookies out of the red-and-white-polka-dot mushroom jar and turned to Mup. "He wouldn't even do sleepovers with Stewart when he was younger because he liked to be in his own bed. We had to drive to the North Shore more than once to pick him up in the middle of the night, remember?"

"But this is why he *should* go. He needs to get pushed out of his comfort zone."

"Eventually, yes," said Mum. "But it's a lot of money. And Paris will be there when he's older, and perhaps more . . . adventurous of spirit?"

They did this sometimes, talking about me in the third person, like I wasn't in the room.

Mup turned to me. "Have you got any money saved from your job?"

"A bit. Not as much as I'd hoped."

"Well, it's a once-in-a-lifetime opportunity. We can manage the deposit. I'll take on some extra Uber shifts." Driving Uber is the second of Mup's three jobs. "I'll write a check tonight. Just don't give it to your teacher till Thursday at the earliest; the funds should be there by then." Mum pursed her lips but said nothing. "And on that note, I'm going to clock a few hours behind the wheel." Mup kissed us both and headed out.

After we'd washed the dishes, Mum let me choose a movie from our massive DVD collection; she buys them for next to nothing at garage sales. I picked our all-time favorite musical, *West Side Story.* We curled up on the couch. Templeton sat on my lap. But, even as we sang along to "Gee, Officer Krupke," I had to fight off the wave of loneliness that was building up inside me.

I was always home on Saturday nights, with one or both of my mothers and my dog. Even Sal had a standing Saturday night date, playing pinochle with a bunch of his age-appropriate friends.

"Are you looking forward to your billet's arrival?" Mum asked during "A Boy Like That."

"Yes." I paused. "I just hope . . ."

"Hope what?"

"I just hope Charlie will like Toronto."

"Of course he will. Why wouldn't he?"

I didn't have the guts to tell her what I was really thinking, which was:

"I hope Charlie will like *me.*"

Like a willow branch
Rippling
And swaying in the breeze

a lune by Wilbur Nuñez-Knopf

"GOOD GOD, BRASS SECTION, YOU SOUND LIKE A BUNCH of dying cats!" Mr. Papadopoulos shouted on Monday over the din, his voice cracking. "Focus!" He waved his baton in the air, revealing massive sweat stains on his red-and-white-checked shirt. His bald head was shiny with sweat.

I stood in the back, concentrating on every note. We were rehearsing "O Canada" one more time before our guests arrived. It didn't require much playing from me except at the end. Anticipating my moment, I stood up. Mr. Papadopoulos looked my way. . . . I picked up my metal beater . . . held my instrument with a bent arm, just below eye level . . . and, on Mr. P's cue, I executed a perfect two-sided roll.

The triangle really is an underappreciated instrument.

* * *

A few minutes later, Mr. P told us to gather up our things and head to the parking lot. I hurried to join Alex—the boy who, for a brief, glorious time, had been my other good friend. Alex had arrived at PET Senior School in mid-September. His mom and dad both worked at the same bank, and they'd been transferred from Calgary to Toronto. Alex is short and round, with thick black hair that falls into his eyes on a constant basis and a mouth full of metal. Back then at least, his clothes made him look like he had an office job: pressed button-up shirt, pressed pants. Everything looked a little too tight for his husky frame. He even carried a briefcase.

In other words, he was a perfect target for Tyler Kertz.

When he took the stool beside me in science class on his first day, I could tell how nervous he was, because he was blinking rapidly and humming tunelessly to himself. Five minutes into class, he dropped his pencil. He hopped off his lab stool, bent down to pick it up—

And tore a hole in his pants with a *riiiiiiiip*, right down the seam of the bum.

A row ahead of us, Tyler swiveled around at the sound, his sharklike senses on high alert; he'd just smelled blood, and he was ready to pounce.

"Excuse me," I blurted. "Beans for dinner last night."

Tyler and some of the other kids looked at me with disgust. "You're so gross, Wank."

I pulled off my beige sweatshirt and handed it to Alex without a word. He tied it around his waist, blinking furiously.

He caught up with me in the hallway after class. "Hey. Thank you. I don't know why you did that, but—thanks." I wasn't sure why I'd done it, either. Maybe I'd decided I had nothing—no dignity, no reputation—left to lose. "Can I give you your sweatshirt back tomorrow?"

"Sure. Of course."

"I'm Alex. Alex Shirazi." He'd smiled up at me. "And I need to buy some bigger pants!" Then he'd burst out laughing, mostly from relief, and he kept on laughing for a long time, until finally I was laughing, too.

After school we realized we were heading the same way, so we walked together, and it turned out we lived a mere two blocks apart. So we started walking to and from PET together, and pretty soon we were hanging out after school, too. I found out that Alex loved watching shows like the late Anthony Bourdain's *Parts Unknown* and other cooking shows like *Chef's Table* and *Salt Fat Acid Heat*. He liked to try to replicate some of the recipes for his parents, and sometimes for me. We discovered we had weird stuff in common, too; like, we both love board games (especially Carcassonne) and we both love a lot of the same music, because our parents brought us up on a similar diet of singer-songwriters like Carole King, Feist, Tom Waits, Cat Power, and a whole bunch of others.

It was like we'd known each other for years, not weeks. In no time we were telling each other the kind of stuff you only share with someone you really trust. Like, he told me about his tics, and how they got bad when he was nervous (and I didn't tell him

I'd already noticed). He told me he'd come out to his parents a year earlier, and at first his dad had been upset, but now he was his biggest advocate; he'd even marched with Alex in Calgary's Pride Parade. I told him all about my time capsule letter, and the aftermath. We made a pact that everything we told each other would stay between us. We even created an elaborate hand-shake to seal the deal: right-hand shake followed by left-hand shake followed by right elbows touching followed by left elbows touching followed by a twirl and a bow.

One night when we were hanging out in his rec room, Alex played me a piece of music on his keyboard. "That was great," I said. "Who wrote it?"

"I did."

"Seriously? That's amazing."

"Thanks. I just wish I could think of lyrics to go with it. But I'm no good at that."

It sounds crazy, but I actually got goosebumps.

The only people who'd read any of my poetry were the Mumps and Sal.

That evening, I let Alex read some of my stuff, too.

The first one he set to music was a poem called "Freefall." "You have to sing," he said. "I can't carry a tune."

At first I refused. Unless I was in the safety of my own home, I never, ever sang out loud.

But Alex persisted. "Of course you can sing in front of me. I'm your friend."

Your. Friend.

So I sang. I know I sucked. But it didn't matter. We just liked the process. Alex set more of my poems to music, and, when we weren't playing Carcassonne or 7 Wonders, we played our songs in the privacy of his basement, to an audience of none.

"We're like Elton John and Bernie Taupin," Alex declared one night, after we'd watched *Rocketman* on Netflix. "Except you're straight and I'm gay."

We had so much fun. In his rec room, we didn't have to worry about the Tylers of the world. Sal was right; having a friend my age was all kinds of awesome. It made the snake pit of high school a bit more bearable.

But as Mup likes to say, "Things that seem too good to be true usually are." One day in early December, Alex locked eyes with Fabrizio Bianchi at band practice, and *boom*—they fell head over heels in love.

I told myself I was happy for him.

But mostly, I was unhappy for me.

Alex was folding up the legs of his keyboard when I approached. "How was your weekend?" I asked.

"Great! Fab and I hung out. I introduced him to Nina Simone. He'd never heard of her before, can you believe it?"

"Wow," I said. "Does he live under a rock? What kind of idiot hasn't heard of Nina Simone?" I attempted a lighthearted laugh.

Alex gave me a wounded look, and even though I towered over him, I suddenly felt much smaller.

Fabrizio strolled over, carrying his trumpet. He's wide and stocky with close-cropped blond hair, and he has a bold fashion sense that some might call cool and others might call a desperate ploy for attention. Even today, he'd added a bright orange scarf to go with our ugly band uniforms. "Hi, Wilbur." He said my name the same way every time, as if he'd heard my pet had just died. He gave me a quick glance up and down, taking in my beige pants and my gray sweatshirt, and pursed his lips like he'd just sucked on a lemon.

He didn't have to say it; if I thought he was a narcissistic attention-seeker, he thought I was a pathetic schlub.

"Hi, Fabrizio. Interesting scarf."

"It's an ascot," he replied.

Please.

"Let's get a move on, people!" Mr. P shouted.

We all headed toward the door. I hoped to get past A Certain Someone unnoticed. Alex and Fabrizio made it past unscathed. Jo Lin, carrying her recorder, got past him, too.

I wasn't so lucky. "Great work today, Frank. That note you played . . . that single, solitary note . . . it really brought everything together. Sheer magic."

Yes. Tyler Kertz is in the band. It is so unfair. Band is supposed to be a refuge for the non-athletic kids; we deserve a safe haven, too. But Kertz is one of those annoying crossovers. Not only is he on the school swim and basketball teams; he also plays saxophone. *And* he's excessively good-looking.

Worst of all, he acts like he's better than the rest of us, like we should be grateful he graces us with his presence. And Mr. P feeds into it, because, well, Tyler *is* a good sax player, and Mr. P thinks he adds a certain panache. But he's also a constant, low-grade jerk. He calls Oliver, the bassoon player, *Oily-ver* because his hair's kind of greasy. Jo Lin is *Ghost* because she's super-shy and quiet. Alex is *Ayatollah* because of his Iranian background. And while Tyler mostly stays away from overtly homophobic digs, he sometimes switches out the *b* in Fabrizio's name for a *g*. He also took way longer than he should have to call Laura—who until last year used a boy's name—by her proper pronoun.

But for some reason, we all take it. Even though we out-number him, twenty-five to one. Maybe we're all just resigned to thinking that this is a microcosm of life, and we might as well get used to it. In my darker moments, I wonder if the others fig-ure that they're the lucky ones; since they don't get it as bad as I do, why rock the boat?

I tried to step around Tyler, but he stepped with me. Then he poked his finger into the soft flesh of my belly. "Is it a boy, or a girl?"

I wanted to kick him in the nuggets. But I don't know how to fight. I couldn't even come up with a good comeback.

So what did I do instead?

I laughed. Like I thought it was funny, too.

And I hated myself almost as much as I hated him.

* * *

We stood outside, waiting for the French students to arrive from the airport. I jumped up and down to stay warm. Even though it was freezing outside, Mr. P had insisted we keep our coats off so our billets would see our band uniforms: black pants paired with orange suit jackets, because orange and black are our school colors. The jackets must have been designed in the eighties, because they have enormous shoulder pads and smell of decades of BO.

"I'm nervous," I said to Alex.

"Me too," he admitted, blinking rapidly.

"I hope they speak English, because I only speak *un poo français.*"

"It's pronounced *peu*," said Fabrizio. *"Un peu français."*

I tried again. *"Poo."*

"Peu."

"Poo."

"Peu."

"That's what I keep saying!"

Alex laughed. "You're right, Wil. You speak poo French."

Suddenly Tyler was beside me. "You might want to stop jumping up and down, Wank. Or get a bra. Your moobs are jiggling."

Poppy, standing nearby, stifled a giggle.

I stopped jumping. Alex gave my hand a quick squeeze.

"I think I see them," said Fabrizio.

A yellow school bus rounded the corner and pulled up to

the curb. As soon as the doors swung open, we started to play "O Canada."

A glamorous woman appeared at the top of the stairs. She wore a gray coat over a red dress, and high heels even though it was cold and snowy. Her hair was pulled into a bun, and her lips matched the color of her dress. Mr. Papadopoulos broke into a big grin and said, "Geneviève! I mean—Mademoiselle Lefèvre! Bonjour!" She was much taller than him, and when they hugged, his head was squished between her breasts. He looked very, very happy.

"Gross," said Fabrizio between notes, and I silently agreed.

When we'd finished "O Canada," the students started spilling out, carrying their instruments. "They look just like us," I said.

"What did you expect?" asked Fab. "That they'd all be wearing berets and carrying wheels of Brie?"

My face turned warm in spite of the cold. "No." But inside I was thinking, *Well, maybe the berets.*

The last student stepped off the bus.

Time slowed. She was tall, almost as tall as me, her brown hair cut in a stylish pageboy. Her shoulders and hips were broad. She wore a yellow faux-fur coat over black-and-white-polka-dot tights, short black boots, and a purple miniskirt. She carried a small guitar case. She wasn't wearing a beret or carrying cheese, but to me, she looked very French. She moved like a cat. Like the Pink Panther. Which is a kind of cat.

She was spectacular.

Mr. Papadopoulos got down to business. "Once you're matched with your billets, you're free to leave with your rides."

"I think the one who looks a bit like Drake is my billet," said Alex.

"I think the tall skinny dude is mine," said Fabrizio.

"I think mine is that guy with the big round head," I said.

Alex and Fab guessed right.

I most definitely did not.

"Charlie Bourget," said Mr. P.

The beautiful girl stepped forward.

My eyes bulged more than usual. "No. You're wrong!"

The beautiful girl arched an eyebrow. "Are you suggesting I do not know my own name?"

"Yes. No. Well, but. You're a girl."

She gave me the most disdainful look anyone has ever given me, and I have been on the receiving end of many disdainful looks. "Charlie. Short for Charlotte."

Mr. Papadopoulos looked flustered. "I'm sorry. I assumed . . ." He scanned his list. "We'll have to figure something out. We can't have a girl billeting with a boy—"

"Why not?" asked Mademoiselle Lefèvre and Charlie in stereo.

"Well." Mr. P cleared his throat. "We don't want anything . . . *untoward* . . . happening."

Alex raised his hand. "Um, sir? By that logic, I shouldn't have a boy billet."

Some of the other students nodded agreement. "You're being awfully heteronormative," added Fabrizio.

"I— No. Whatever that means, I am not—"

"And possibly transphobic," added Laura.

"I am none of those things," said Mr. P. "The rest of you marked that you have separate bedrooms for your billets. Mr. Nuñez-Knopf does not. *That* is why I'm raising this—"

"Where is Mademoiselle Lefèvre staying, sir?" asked Fabrizio innocently.

"I—she's—she's staying in my apartment."

"And she has her own room?"

Mr. P's entire face turned pink. His mouth opened. Closed. Opened again.

Charlie was starting to shiver from the cold. *"Mon Dieu."* She looked me in the eye. "You. Boy. Will you be, how did he say it, *untoward*?"

"N-no," I stammered. "I'm not that kind of man."

"See?" said Charlie. "He is gay. So it is no problem."

"Of course," said Mr. P. "I should have realized."

"I'm not gay," I said. "But I was raised by two awesome gay women who've nurtured my feminine side, so perhaps that's what you're picking up on—"

"Okay, alors. It is settled," interrupted Mademoiselle Lefèvre. "We are all tired and want to get out of the cold. Charlotte will stay with the nice homosexual."

Tyler was doubled over with laughter.

And I wanted to run away as fast as my tree-trunk legs would carry me.

Mrs. Shirazi had offered to pick Charlie and me up along with Alex and his billet, Léo, and Fabrizio and his billet, Christophe, since the Mumps were both working. She gave me two air kisses, left cheek, right cheek. I could smell her perfume. "Wilbur, hello. How are you and your mothers?"

"We're good," I said. "And you and Mr. Shirazi?"

"Oh, just fine. We haven't seen much of you lately."

Because your son has abandoned his friend for his boyfriend, I wanted to say.

We piled into their minivan. Charlie, Fabrizio, and I squished into the back. Charlie immediately fell asleep, her head against the window. Her mouth hung open and a bit of saliva pooled in one corner. She had a splash of freckles around her nose, and big nostrils. Her ears were a bit sticky-outy.

She was just . . . *wow.*

Fabrizio elbowed me, hard. "Quit staring," he whispered. "It's creepy."

Alex was already talking in a mix of French and English to Léo and Christophe. I envied how much more comfortable he seemed in his own skin since he'd started dating Fabrizio; I would have given anything to exchange mine, just turn in my entire epidermis for a new one.

Charlie and I were dropped off first. Since we were in the back, everyone had to get out. I grabbed Alex's arm. "This is the worst thing that's happened to me in my entire life," I hissed.

"Really? How so?"

"Seriously, I don't think I can do this. She's gorgeous."

"I wouldn't go that far," said Fabrizio, eavesdropping.

"Was I talking to you?" I turned my back on him. "Alex, seriously: Could we switch?"

"Wilbur. You'll be fine." Alex took Charlie's suitcase from the back and handed it to me. "Just be yourself."

"Well, not *too* much yourself," said Fabrizio, *still* eavesdropping.

Then the two of them hopped back into the minivan, and Mrs. Shirazi drove away, leaving me all alone with Charlie.

She waited for me on the sidewalk. "Um. *Je m'excuse*," I began in a loud voice. "*Je*, um, speak . . . *poo français*."

"I am not hard of hearing, or stupid," she replied. "You do not need to shout. My English is much, much better than your French."

"Oh. Okay."

"This is a very interesting neighborhood, yes? Lots of murals and graffiti and sculptures made from *objets trouvés*." She watched a woman skip past in head-to-toe tie-dye clothing, followed by a Rastafarian. "And people from all walks of life. Like Christiania in Copenhagen."

"Sure," I replied, even though I had no idea what she was

talking about because I have never traveled anywhere. I took her suitcase and she took her instrument case. We headed up the front walk. I tried to think of something, anything, to say. "That's a tiny guitar."

"It is not a guitar. It is a ukulele."

"You play ukulele?"

"No, I just carry it with me as part of my look."

"Oh. You pull it off very well—"

"I am joking, Wilbur. Of course I play it."

"Ah. Right. Ha-ha." I made a mental note that the French did sarcasm, too.

"What instrument do you play?"

"Triangle."

Her brow furrowed. "As in, *ding*?" She mimed the movement.

"I also play cowbell and tambourine."

"Ah. A triple threat." I couldn't tell whether or not she was being sarcastic again.

Templeton practically launched himself at us when I opened the front door. He started running in circles around Charlie on his stubby legs, yapping happily.

"A Chihuahua, *non?*"

"Chihuahua-dachshund mix."

"He is possibly the ugliest dog I have ever seen." She only stated the truth, so it was hard to take offense. Templeton is nine, which is fifty-two in human years. I think his fur was originally white, but now it's yellow, like a smoker's fingers. He has a snaggletooth, he's blind in one eye, and he's missing an ear. It's just one more reason why I love him so much, because I'm not the most attractive specimen, either. Mup says we're both beautiful on the inside, which, now that I think of it, is not actually a compliment.

"I like to think he's so ugly, he's cute," I said.

"It is not cute that he is having sex with my leg."

"Templeton, stop! Bad dog." I scooped him up. Charlie hung her coat on one of the colorful hooks in the hallway while I knocked three times on the wall.

"Why did you do that?"

"My best friend. We have a system. When I get home from school, I knock. If he doesn't knock back, I call him. If he doesn't answer his phone, I go over with my spare key. Just in case he's fallen or something like that."

"What is wrong with him that he might fall?"

"Nothing. Just old age."

On cue, Sal knocked back: one, two, three.

Charlie glanced into our living room, and my heart constricted just a bit. After our avalanche of bad luck, we'd had to find creative ways to furnish the house. Mum and I had completely outfitted our home with what she and I call collectibles and Mup calls trash. I think it gives our house a homey look. Mup thinks it gives it a hoarder look. "Does one man's junk *always* have to be your treasure?" Mup says every time a new item makes it into our space.

So I watched with bated breath as Charlie took in the old purple couch, the hot-pink velvet chaise longue, the lamp with the gold tasseled shade, the kidney-shaped coffee table, and all the knickknacks and doodads Mum and I had picked up over the last few years, like the salt-and-pepper-shaker collection that lined the mantle and the old framed advertisements that hung on the wall.

"Eclectic design," she said with an approving nod. "I like it."

This made me inordinately happy.

We each took one end of her suitcase and carried it up the narrow stairs to the second floor. When we stepped into my room, my happy feeling vanished. Why hadn't I taken down my old Emma Watson poster? Yes, she's a super-smart feminist, but my poster was from the first Harry Potter movie; she was in her Hogwarts robes, wielding her wand. Even my favorite garage-sale find, a painting of dogs playing poker, suddenly seemed ridiculous under her Parisian gaze. "You can have the bed," I said. "I'll sleep in the alcove." My room has a unique shape, with a smaller separate crawl space under the eaves. Mup and I had put an air mattress in there the night before. "I emptied the top two drawers of my dresser. Is there anything else you need?"

She didn't answer. Her gaze had landed on my bedside table.

Lying there in full view: Latex gloves. Kleenex. Petroleum jelly.

Her brow furrowed. She looked at me, alarmed.

It took me a moment.

"No! You don't— I swear it's not for— It's for Templeton! My dog!"

"*Quoi?*"

"For expressing his anal sacs. It's a condition some dogs get. We can't afford to take him to the vet all the time, so I learned how to do it at home." She looked at me blankly, and I could tell I'd lost her. "I just put on the gloves"—I pantomimed putting on the gloves—"then I use a bit of the jelly"—I pantomimed putting jelly on my finger—"then I poke my finger up his rectum, find the anal sacs, and squeeze the contents onto the Kleenex. . . ." I pantomimed that part, too.

"You are a lover of animals."

"Yes! Yes, I am a lover of animals."

She bolted out of my room and down the stairs.

A moment later, I heard her scream.

I guess I would have screamed too if I'd come face to face with a zombie. Charlie had been punching in Mademoiselle Lefèvre's number on her phone when Mum walked through the door, straight from a movie set that she called "the poor man's *Walking Dead.*" The makeup artist had gone all out; it really did look as if half of her face had rotted away.

Luckily, Mum speaks decent French, so she was able to calm Charlie down pretty quickly. A few minutes later the two of them were laughing in the kitchen while Mum put the kettle on.

"Oh, Wil," Mum said. "First she thought you were a serial masturbator. Then she thought you were diddling the dog!" I tried to laugh, but I was pretty offended.

As if I would ever diddle the dog.

Sal sent me a text while Charlie and I set the table for dinner.

How is your excellent stud?

Sal hates thumb-typing, and his eyesight isn't the best, so sometimes I have to decipher the spelling mistakes and autocorrects.

My exchange student is a girl. Charlie = Charlotte.

Like your favorite spider! Sal responded.

Sal and I often did book swaps, and I'd recently loaned him my much-loved copy of *Charlotte's Web*.

But prettier, I typed. And without eight eyes and legs.

Thank goofiness for that.

Want to come to dinner?

Who's cooking?

Norah.

. . .

Think I'll eat here, thanks.

Sal likes Mum's cooking as much as the rest of us.

Mup arrived home just as we sat down to dinner. She was wearing work pants and an old sweater, and she was covered in tufts of fur. "Stanley and Daisy were hellions today," she said.

"You work with children?" asked Charlie.

"Dogs. Which is almost the same thing. Except most children are toilet trained." Mup works at a doggy daycare a few days a week—her third of three jobs.

I relaxed during supper because I knew the Mumps would carry the conversation. Templeton lay at my feet, hoping for scraps. Mum, her makeup removed and her sweatpants on, served us one of her specialties, a meatless meatloaf.

"I got bumped up to *special skills* extra on set today," she told us. "The director shot me in close-up, chewing off someone's arm. I got to say, 'Aaaaaaaaaaagh.'"

"Very convincing," I said.

"It sent a chill up my spine," Charlie agreed.

"Tell us more about you, Charlie," said Mup. "Do you have brothers and sisters?"

"*Non.* I am an only child, like Wilbur. I live with my father."

"And your mother . . . ?"

"She is not with us."

I put down my fork. A lump rose in my throat. I worried I might cry, because this was a million times sadder than the Sarah McLachlan song. "I'm so sorry," I said. "When did she . . . ?"

"When I was seven."

"How did she . . . ?" asked Mup.

"A train."

All three of us tried to keep our horror in check. "She got hit by a train?" I asked.

Charlie looked puzzled. Then she started to laugh. "Oh—*non*! I have not explained well. When I was seven, she took a train to the South of France with her boyfriend! She is alive."

We all exhaled. "Thank goodness," said Mum. Then: "Why didn't she take you with her?"

"She said she had to follow her heart. I spend summers with her."

The Mumps looked horrified all over again. I tried to imagine how I would feel if one of them left to "follow her heart." It was too sad to contemplate.

Mum brought down the carousel cookie jar and put out a plate of her quinoa squares. "You must eat a lot of cookies in this house," Charlie said, checking out the twenty or so jars that lined the tops of the cupboards.

"Nope," said Mup. "We just live with a hoard—forgive me, a *collector*."

"They make me happy," said Mum. "What does your father do, Charlie?" she asked, changing the subject.

"He is an intellectual."

"I mean, what does he do for a job?"

"Just that."

Mup whistled. "Wow. I don't think *intellectual* is a job description in North America. Over here, when someone is called an intellectual, it's an insult. Especially if you're a politician."

"But that makes no sense," said Charlie. "You want your politicians to be smart, *non*?"

Mum gave a sad smile. "You would think so, wouldn't you?"

"In France, we value the knowledgeable person's opinion." Charlie took a bite from a quinoa square. Her eyes widened. A moment later, I saw her drop the rest of the square on the floor for Templeton, who gobbled it up because he will eat literally anything, including but not limited to cigarette butts, dirty underpants, and his own barf.

"What does he do, exactly?" I asked.

"He writes for newspapers and magazines. He publishes essays. And he appears often on TV. My father and I, we argue all the time, but not in a bad way. He wants me to be a critical thinker."

I nodded and tried to look like I might be thinking critically. But what was going through my head was *She is out of my league in every way.*

* * *

After dinner Charlie said she'd like to join Templeton and me on our evening walk, and I felt anxious all over again. I put Templeton into the rainbow-colored sweater Mum had knit for him and slid four little matching booties onto his feet. We headed out into the freezing cold night.

"Please, will you take me to get something to eat?" Charlie said. "Your mothers are wonderful, but *mon Dieu,* that meatless meatloaf . . ."

"Was revolting?"

"*Oui!* I do not want to starve to death on my first trip to Canada."

"I promise I won't let that happen. The Mumps have many great qualities, but cooking isn't top of the list, especially for Mum." We started walking east toward the heart of the market.

"Why do you call them that? The Mumps?"

I shrugged. "When I was really little, I started calling Norah *Mum,* and Carmen *Mup.* Put them together and they make the Mumps."

"I like it." She was shivering; her yellow faux-fur coat wasn't enough protection from the cold. "I can see my breath!" She puffed out her cheeks and blew little clouds of air.

The Jamaican patty shop was still open, so I took her inside. She bought three beef patties and wolfed them down. She was a noisy eater, groaning with delight and chewing loudly. Lloyd winked at me. "Gotta love a woman with an appetite."

"*Délicieux!*" Charlie declared when she was done. Lloyd seemed pleased. We said goodbye and headed back outside.

Charlie was still hungry, so I took her to the corner store. She bought some beef jerky and a Mars bar and wolfed those down, too.

"I thought French people didn't eat junk food."

"Oh, no. We love our junk food just as much as you Americans."

"Canadians."

"American, Canadian. It is the same thing, no?"

"No. It is not the same thing, not at all—"

She burst out laughing. "I am joking! I told a joke in English. I am very good."

And very beautiful, I thought, *even with all that beef and chocolate stuck in your teeth.*

I untied Templeton's leash from a signpost. He peed against a fire hydrant. Charlie bent down and gave him her last piece of jerky; he inhaled it. "How long have you had this strange little creature?"

"I got him just over a year ago, at Christmas."

"He was a present?"

"Not really, no. I volunteered at the animal shelter over the break." Just thinking of that Christmas brought on a residual wave of sadness. Mup's dad—her last surviving parent, and technically my grandfather, although I'd never met him—had died just before the holidays. She'd flown to Buenos Aires for the funeral, even though he had disowned her when she'd come out. The flight had blown our Christmas budget, and the trip left her depressed. The mood in the house was bleak. To top it off, Sal had gone on a monthlong trip with Friendship Force to Australia, so I couldn't escape to his house, and Alex wasn't even in the picture yet. So when I'd heard the SPCA needed dog walkers to fill in for vacationing volunteers, I leapt at the chance. "Templeton was in the very last cage," I told Charlie. "He was a mess. I don't know what had happened to him in his last home, but he looked like he'd just given up."

Charlie knelt down to pet Templeton's head, and he made a purring sound. *"Pauvre petit."*

"No one was interested in adopting him. He was going to be euthanized in a few days. So I decided that those days should be good ones. I took him for a walk every morning. And he was so sweet and so grateful. . . . He'd look at me with his one good eye and smile—"

"Smile?"

"He smiles. I swear. The day before he was scheduled to die, I couldn't take it. I walked him back to our place and begged the Mumps to let me keep him."

The three of us began to walk back home. There was a crescent moon in the sky.

"Wilbur, that is a beautiful story. You saved Templeton's life."

I didn't tell Charlie that, as far as I was concerned, it was the other way around.

Falling for her
Helpless to fight it
Charlotte's the match
And now it's ignited

From "The Match," by Wilbur Nuñez-Knopf

"WILBUR, WAKE UP!" I OPENED MY EYES TO THE SOUND of Charlie's voice, sat up too fast, and hit my head.

Right. Air mattress. Alcove. Templeton, snoozing and farting at my feet.

"You must come and see!"

When I stepped around the corner, Charlie was sitting in the bay window, wearing blue-and-white-striped men's pajamas. Her nose was pressed to the glass, like she was a little kid. "Look!"

I peered outside. It had snowed during the night. Our street was blanketed in white. "It is so beautiful," she said.

"Yes," I said, looking at her. "Beautiful."

The Mumps had bought bagels and cream cheese from NU Bügel. Charlie wolfed down two of them and drank three cups of black coffee. She'd changed into a long white sweater, which she wore over another pair of cool tights; these ones had cat faces all over them. A pink-and-purple scarf was wrapped artfully around her neck. Her only makeup was bright red lipstick. She was not what anyone would call a traditional beauty; her nose was almost as large as mine, and her eyebrows were thick and furry like mine, too. But when you put the pieces together, they clicked.

She was like a tropical bird. A flamingo, maybe, or a toucan. She was so . . . *colorful.*

I, on the other hand, wore my standard gray sweatshirt and baggy beige pants. I'd long ago gotten rid of anything that made me stand out in any way, including my beloved Tilley hat.

I stifled yawns between mouthfuls of bagel. I'd barely slept. I was terrified that I'd fart in my sleep and stink up the room, because as a vegetarian I do eat a lot of legumes; Sal says I'm the gassiest person he's ever met. Then, when I'd finally started to drift off, I was wakened by a snorting sound. At first I thought it was Templeton. But it was Charlie, snoring loudly in her sleep.

When I was done with my breakfast, I left Charlie to discuss politics with Mum while I went outside to shovel snow. Once I'd done our walkway, I started on Sal's. It was slow work, because I needed to stop every few minutes to rescue Templeton, whose long, low-to-the-ground body kept disappearing in the fresh snow.

Sal's door opened as I reached the stairs to his porch. "Well? Where is she?" He was dressed for the day, looking dapper as always in a sweater vest and brown trousers, his favorite fuzzy pink slippers on his feet.

I was about to answer when suddenly, *whack!* I was hit in the side of the head with a snowball.

"Sorry! I could not resist!" It was Charlie, standing on our front porch. She'd traded her yellow faux-fur coat for Mum's orange parka, which she'd bought for standing around outside on movie sets. "Your mother loaned me this coat. Now I feel like a fresh-baked baguette!"

I wiped a blob of snow from my ear. "Sal, this is my billet, Charlie. Charlie, this is my neighbor and best friend, Sal Goldstein."

"The man who knocks." She extended her mittened hand. "It is very nice to meet you, Mr. Goldstein. I promise I will not throw snow at you."

"Much obliged. And please, call me Sal." I noticed that he didn't immediately take her hand. "What are your views on the Vichy government?"

I had no idea what that was, but Charlie clearly did, because she hocked a loogie into the snow. "I spit on the Vichy government! My great-grandparents on my father's side fought for the Resistance."

Sal's face relaxed into a grin. He took her mittened hand, raised it to his lips, and kissed it. "In that case . . . *enchanté.*"

* * *

"Why do you think he asked me about the Vichy government?" Charlie asked as we headed to school.

"Um. What exactly is that, again?" I tried to sound like I knew but had temporarily forgotten.

"It was the puppet government in France during World War II. They collaborated with the Nazis. It is a stain on our history." She scooped up some fresh snow and licked it with her tongue. "I guess Sal might have been alive during that time?"

"He was." I told her what I knew of Sal's story, which wasn't much, because he didn't like to talk about it. "He was born in Germany. When he was really little, his parents were sent to a concentration camp for being 'political dissidents.' He never saw them again."

"Wilbur. That is terrible," she said.

"I know. I can't even imagine."

"What happened to him?"

"Friends of his parents managed to get him on a *Kindertransport* to England. He lived with a family on a farm throughout the war. When he was sixteen, he made his way to Canada on a merchant marine ship." I shook my head. "He didn't know anyone. He hardly had any education. But he built a life for himself. He's the most courageous person I've ever met. And also the most positive."

"You are lucky to have him as a friend."

"Very."

We met up with Alex and Léo at the corner of College and

Augusta. Charlie and Léo got caught up in French, so Alex and I had a chance to check in. "How was your first night?" I asked.

"Great! Léo's teaching me all the swears in French. And he likes to cook too, so we made the pasta all'uovo from *Salt Fat Acid Heat*. He wants me to teach him how to cook Persian food. How about you?"

"Stressful. I've never slept with a woman before."

"You still haven't—"

"I mean, aside from sleeping in between Mum and Mup until I was five."

Alex made a face. "See now, that's the sort of thing you can say to me if you must. But don't say it to anyone else."

"Gotcha."

The four of us headed north on Huron Street, winding our way through the University of Toronto campus to get to our school, which was just north of Bloor. We picked up Fabrizio and Christophe along the way. Mr. P had told us all to gather in the band room, and we spent the morning playing our repertoire for each other. One of our numbers was "Play That Funky Music" by Wild Cherry, which gave me a chance to showcase my cowbell skills.

When we were done, the French students played for us. Mademoiselle Lefèvre explained that Paris schools don't have bands, so she'd formed this group through a conservatory. "We are called *Les Jeunes de Paris*."

They had a few brass instruments and lots of strings: guitars, a banjo, and Charlie's ukulele. I guess I thought that, being from Europe, they'd play a lot of classical music. But they played mostly pop songs; my favorite was David Bowie's "Space Oddity."

Charlie was amazing. I couldn't keep my eyes off her. She stuck her tongue out just a bit while she was playing.

At one point, though, I noticed that I wasn't the only one watching her.

Tyler Kertz was watching her, too.

Correction:

He was watching *me* watching her, *then* he was watching her . . .

Which made the whole thing feel that much worse.

He swooped in as we headed down to the Art Gallery of Ontario after lunch. Charlie and I were walking side by side, chatting about the acting classes she took once a week back home. "We start with exercises. Like, we lie on the floor and pretend we are sponges, filling up with water," she was saying, when suddenly I was elbowed right off the sidewalk and into a pile of slush.

"Charlotte, we haven't properly met. I'm Tyler," he said, flashing a pearly white smile.

Charlie smiled. "Has anyone ever told you you look like Chris Hemsworth?"

He ducked his head, like he was embarrassed. "I've heard that once or twice. I'm sure you get told all the time that you look like Emma Stone?"

Barf! It was just so *phony!* I waited for Charlie to slay him with one of her disdainful looks.

But she didn't. Not even close.

She *blushed*. "Oh! No. I do not believe you, but *merci*."

He chatted her up the rest of the way, while I trailed after them like a sad puppy.

The moment we stepped inside the AGO, Alex said, "Come with me to the washroom."

"But I don't have to—"

"Not a request." He grabbed my arm and pulled me into the men's. He checked under the stalls to make sure we were alone. "You like her, don't you? As in, *like her,* like her."

"Is it that obvious?"

"No. I mean, only to people with eyes." He started to laugh. Alex's laugh is normally highly infectious, but this time I just couldn't join in.

"It's so dumb. As if I'd ever stand a chance."

"Why do you say that?"

"Because. Look at her. Then look at me."

We both studied my reflection in the mirror. "It's true that you're not classically handsome," said Alex.

"Is that supposed to make me feel better, because so far, so bad—"

"Let me finish. I was going to say, you have *character*. And character matters. My mom says it's why she fell in love with my dad. In case you haven't noticed, she's *way* better looking than him." He spoke the truth; Mr. Shirazi liked to say that Mrs. Shirazi looked like a Persian Salma Hayek while he looked like a Persian Danny DeVito. "And I'm shaped like a meatball," Alex continued. "A meatball with a mouthful of metal! But Fabrizio thinks I'm awesome, even though he's way better looking than me—"

"Patently untrue, aside from the fact that you're awesome—"

"My point is, he likes me for *me*. Maybe the same can be true for you and Charlie."

I felt a brief flicker of optimism; then I remembered: "I think Tyler likes her. And I think he only likes her because *I* like her."

"Ugh, he's such a jerk." He thought about it for a moment. "But you know what? You still have the advantage. Because *you* get to spend twenty-four–seven with her. Not him. *You*."

I looked down at him, because he's ten inches shorter than me, and smiled. "Thanks, Alex."

"You're welcome, Wil." Then he initiated our secret handshake.

It was just like old times.

When it was time to leave the gallery, we couldn't find Mr. P or Mademoiselle Lefèvre anywhere. Laura was just about to have them called on the PA system, when the door to the all-access washroom opened, and they stepped out. Mademoiselle Lefèvre's hair was mussed, and the buttons on Mr. P's shirt were done up crooked. "That is just all kinds of wrong," muttered Fabrizio.

Alex was going to Fabrizio's with their billets, so Charlie and I walked home just the two of us, through a bustling Chinatown and into Kensington Market. The sky was a vibrant blue, and the snow was starting to melt.

"I need to get Templeton out for a walk," I said. "He's been home all day. Come to think of it, I should get Sal out for a walk, too. He doesn't like going out by himself after a heavy snowfall."

"I will come with you. We will walk them both."

Templeton and Sal were both delighted to get out. The four of us slow-walked through the market. Charlie held Templeton's leash, Sal held his cane, and I held Sal's arm.

"Mmm, the food looks so good," said Charlie as we walked past the cheese shops, bakeries, butchers, fishmongers, and produce stores.

"Wilbur and I know where to get all the free samples," Sal told her. "If you're interested."

"Oh, please! I am always hungry. My father thinks I have a—how do you call it? A tapeworm."

We started in Viktor's cheese shop. He let us try six different types of cheese before telling us to move along. The bakery had a tray of brownie samples sitting on the counter; we ate them all. Then Brenda, the woman behind the counter, gave Sal a giant cookie because she thinks he is "adorable and looks like Leonard Cohen." He shared it with us once we'd left the shop. We sampled a gross green smoothie and eight flavors of ice cream, too. In between sampling, Sal and Charlie talked about Paris. "I know your city well. My wife, Irma, and I went there for our honeymoon, and every ten years after that. Six times in total."

They spoke in a mixture of English and French (because speaking three languages fluently is another one of Sal's skills), and I mostly zoned out, happy to just be in the moment with my best friend, my awesome dog, and a fabulous girl.

Charlie burped as we reached the far end of the market. "*Now* I am full," she said. "Can we invite Sal for dinner?"

"I have supper at Wilbur's on Wednesdays and Sundays," Sal told her. "But tonight, I have a standing date with my bowling buddies."

"Sal is extremely popular," I said.

We dropped him off at his place. As we headed down his walk, then up ours, Charlie linked arms with me. "Has anyone ever told you you look like that boy in that old movie? Napoleon Dynamite. Only with bigger eyes. And dark hair instead of blond."

"N-no," I stammered, absorbing the compliment. I hadn't seen the movie, but if she was talking about an actor, I figured he had to be good-looking.

I felt happy, and not the type of happy I felt when I was with Sal, or Alex, but a special, heart-expanding happy, reserved just for Charlie.

The feeling lasted until that evening, when the Mumps threatened to ruin it all.

Mothers, Smothers
I love you with all my might
But I sometimes wish the umbilical cord
Wasn't wrapped so tight

From "Smothers" by Wilbur Nuñez-Knopf

MUP COOKED DINNER THAT NIGHT, WHICH WAS A RELIEF. She made a Tex-Mex casserole. Charlie had three servings.

After we'd cleared away the dishes, the Mumps pulled out the karaoke machine. They got things started by singing a duet of "Don't Go Breaking My Heart" by Elton John and Kiki Dee. It was an ancient machine, with music to match. Then Charlie got up and sang a song called "Poison Arrow" by ABC. She was a truly awful singer; but what she lacked in ability, she made up for in sheer enthusiasm. "I take theater lessons in Paris," she told the Mumps when she was done. "And whenever we put on a musical, I know I will have a very small part!" Then she laughed. I'd never met someone so completely, cheerfully comfortable with their absence of talent.

"Now you sing, Wilbur," she said, grabbing me by the arm and pulling me to my feet.

"Sorry, can't. Templeton needs his evening walk." There was no way on earth that I would intentionally humiliate myself in front of *anyone*, let alone her.

The temperatures had plunged again, so Templeton and I only walked a few blocks before he sat down in the middle of the sidewalk and refused to go any farther. I wound up carrying him home while he licked my face and smiled at me, looking awfully pleased with himself.

When we got back inside, the karaoke machine had been put away. Charlie was sitting on our purple couch in between Mum and Mup, directly underneath a framed ad of a stylish 1960s woman in a pillbox hat, bright red roses in the foreground, with the tagline *Kotex is confidence*.

Laid out on the coffee table was a familiar-looking, bulging scrapbook.

No. Please, no.

Mup caught my eye and gave me an apologetic look. "Charlie saw it and pulled it off the shelf." Mum, however, was completely absorbed, clearly enjoying this opportunity to take a trip down memory lane.

"Wilbur, you were such an adorable little boy!" said Charlie. "You are naked in almost all of these photos."

Kill me now.

"He loved being unencumbered." Mum smiled fondly. "He'd rip off all his clothes the moment he walked through the front door, no matter the season."

Mup mouthed, *Sorry.* I bent down to peel off Templeton's booties, hoping to hide my tomato-red face.

"We used to joke that his favorite suit was his birthday suit, didn't we, Carmen?"

Mup, bless her heart, leaned over and turned the page.

"Here he is screaming blue murder at his first-ever haircut," said Mum. "And again on the back of one of those automated supermarket horses . . . oh, and again at the Raffi concert. 'Bananaphone' gave him conniptions for some reason. Such a sweet, sensitive little boy."

"Maybe it's time for dessert," said Mup—but Charlie had turned the page again.

"What are these?" She pointed at some letters that had been glued into the album.

Mum made a face. "We don't need to talk about those—"

"Oh yes, let's," said Mup, suddenly enjoying herself. "Let's talk about those."

Mum sighed. "They are my shame. But Carmen says you can't erase history, so they've been included."

"Have you read *Charlotte's Web* by E. B. White?" asked Mup.

"Non."

"It's a famous children's story on this side of the pond. And it was Wil's absolute favorite book. It's about a friendship that forms between a pig and a spider. Norah first read it to him when he was six."

"Oh, how he loved the story, and especially the spider, Charlotte!" said Mum. "She was your first crush, wasn't she, Wil?"

"Mum—"

"He would lean against me with his thumb in his mouth while I read, and one day he said, 'I love Charlotte. I'm going to marry her.' It was the sweetest thing. But, in the story, Charlotte dies. And the closer I got to the end, the more I thought, there is no way Wil can handle this, not yet—"

"So she engaged in blatant censorship," Mup interjected. "We have an expression in English: *helicopter parent*—"

"As I've pointed out many times, Carmen, it wasn't censorship. It was *creative editing*."

"You say potato," said Mup. "She gave the story a different ending. In her version, the spider and the pig get married and live happily ever after in the barn."

Charlie's furry eyebrows shot up in surprise. "In France, we would never shield children from the realities of life or change an author's work."

Mum tried to explain. "I know how it sounds. But you have to understand, Wil was an emotionally fragile little boy. He felt things in a big way."

Mup opened her mouth, and for one optimistic moment I thought she might come to my rescue. "He'd cry if we killed a mosquito."

My optimism was unfounded.

"One day, Wil handed Norah a sheet of paper," Mup con-

74

tinued. She picked up the scrapbook and showed it to Charlie. "He'd written a letter to the author, E. B. White."

> *"Deer Mr. E. B. White, I hop you are well. You are my favorite wrighter. I love* Charlotte's Web *it is the best book in all the univers and my mum has red it to me five times. I wuz scared in parts like what wood happen to Wilbur the pig but then I wuz happy becuz the spider helped him she wuz such a good frend. And then they got merried! Do you have frends? Or bruthers and sisters? I am an only child and I sumtimes wish I had a bruther or sister becuz I dunt have a lot of frends. Anyway thanks for wrighting such a beetiful story.*
>
> *Please wright back I wood luv to here from you Mr. E. B. White my favorite wrighter.*
>
> *Luv, William"*

"That is a very sweet letter," Charlie said when Mup was done. "But why is it signed *William*?"

Mum cleared her throat. "Maybe we'll let Wil explain that one."

Charlie looked at me. I sighed. "*William* is the name on my birth certificate." I felt the heat rise in my face again. "But when I was ten, I decided I wanted to be called Wilbur."

"After," Charlie began—

"*A pig,*" Mup said.

75

"You both called me *Wil* anyway," I said defensively. "I didn't think it would be a big deal."

But it *was* a big deal. The Mumps kept trying to convince me to change it back; I kept refusing. I heard Mup one night, talking to Mum: "He changed his name to a barnyard animal! A *pig*, no less. A pig who isn't even the hero of the story. It's *Charlotte's Web*, not . . . *Wilbur's Sty*. He's making himself a secondary character *in his own life*." I couldn't believe how thoroughly they'd missed the point. Charlotte had written really nice things about Wilbur in her web to help keep him from the slaughterhouse. Things like, "Some pig!" and "Terrific!" and "Radiant!"

I wanted to be all of those things, too.

"What happened with the letter?" asked Charlie. "Did you mail it?"

"I couldn't," said Mum. "E. B. White died in 1985."

"And Norah didn't want to tell him that, either," said Mup. "So she *pretended* to mail the letter."

"You're making it sound worse than it was," Mum protested.

"I am making it sound exactly the way it was. Norah realized he'd be crushed if he didn't get a response. So she wrote back." Mup flipped to the next page of the album and read aloud.

"Dear William, thank you so much for writing to me. I am delighted to hear that Charlotte's Web *is your favorite book. I had a lot of fun writing it. I don't have a lot of friends either because I am quite shy, and I prefer to spend my time in the countryside with my family and*

my dachshund. I am happy to be your pen pal and long-distance friend. I can help you with your spelling too because it looks like you need it, ha-ha!

Sincerely,
Mr. E. B. White."

Mup flipped through page after page of letters in the album. "Their correspondence went on for two years, until Wil decided to read the book on his own when he was nine."

"He was just gutted when he got to the part where Charlotte dies," said Mum.

"And equally gutted that my own mother had lied to me for two long years," I added pointedly.

"I don't see how it's all that different from, say, Santa Claus, or the Easter Bunny—"

"What is this drawing?" asked Charlie. She'd flipped to the final page of the album.

"Nothing—" I began.

But Mup was already laughing at the memory. "Wil drew that. He'd been asking us who his daddy was. We told him we'd got a sperm donor for Mum."

Mum started laughing, too. "The next day he handed us this drawing. We asked what it was."

"And he said"—Mup had to stop, she was laughing so hard—"it's a picture of Mummy—eating a sperm doughnut." They both lost it.

It took Charlie a moment to translate from English to French in her head—then she too burst out laughing. They were all doubled over, snorting with pleasure at my expense.

I stood up. "Goodnight!" I said it louder than I meant to.

Mum stopped laughing long enough to say, "But, pickle, it's only nine o'clock—"

"I agree with you both that we need to tear down the patriarchy," I said, trying hard to keep my voice level, "but right now, I've had it up to my eyeballs with the matriarchy." I strode stoically out of the room and up the stairs. Charlie's furry eyebrows shot up again in surprise. Templeton, bless his heart, barked angrily at the Mumps before he scrambled after me. But his legs are short, and his body is low, and he can't get up the stairs on his own. So I had to come back down, lift him into my arms, and stride stoically back up again.

It didn't feel quite as impactful the second time around.

Charlie came in a while later, dressed for bed in her blue-and-white-striped pajamas. I could hear her moving around from my alcove.

Neither of us said a word as she settled in. She was quiet for so long, I assumed she'd fallen asleep. Then she said into the darkness, "I think it is crazy that Norah changed the ending to that story and wrote letters to you from a dead man. My father believes that children should always be told the truth, even if it is upsetting."

"Your dad sounds like a smart man." I paused. "Which makes sense. Since he's an intellectual."

"Those letters you wrote . . . they were so wonderful. What a sweet little boy you were. You loved animals even then. That is a very good quality in a man."

"I guess."

"I could tell that you were angry with your mothers tonight. But, Wilbur. Those stories they told . . . they did it out of love. And I know they were laughing, but only in the way that people can laugh when they love someone so deeply."

"If you say so."

"I am very envious of your relationship with your mothers. They adore you."

That was a fact I could not deny.

It was quiet again.

Then I heard a strange sniffling sound.

"Charlie? Are you crying?"

There was a pause. *"Oui."*

I poked my head around the alcove. She wasn't in bed; she was sitting in the window seat, looking out at the night. I got up and sat down at the other end. We both had our knees up close to our chins; our toes were almost touching. "What's making you sad?"

"I lied when I said I didn't miss my mother. I feel much anger at her a lot of the time. And her boyfriend is much younger than her, and he is such a terrible little—how do you say? *Turd.* I can't believe she left me and my father for him. Especially me, her only child."

"It's hard to understand. Particularly because you must have been the most amazing kid."

"Oh, Wilbur. *Merci.*"

"Would you like Templeton to sleep with you tonight?"

"Really?"

"Of course." I put Templeton on the end of her bed. "Stay," I said to him. Then I crawled back onto my air mattress in the alcove. A few moments passed.

"*Pew.* He has very bad gas," said Charlie.

"Would you like me to take him back?"

"*Non.* Please don't. I like having him here." Then another "Pew!"

I didn't tell her that it wasn't Templeton. I do a lot for him; it's only fair that, once in a while, he can be my fall guy.

Birds sing, hope springs
Skies are blue above
Everything is beautiful
When you realize you're in love

From "Love," by Wilbur Nuñez-Knopf

WE GOT TO BE TOURISTS IN OUR OWN CITY FOR THE EN-
tire week, all paid for by our school's Parent Action Committee.
I saw places I'd never been to before because the Mumps could
never afford them, like Casa Loma, the zoo, Fort York, the Aga
Khan Museum, and even the Bata Shoe Museum.

I also found out a lot about Charlie. (1) She was born in
January, making her almost a full year older than me—an older
woman! (2) She did not currently have a boyfriend and hadn't
for a while. (3) She once performed in an all-female production
of *Glengarry Glen Ross,* in French, and a total of thirteen people
came over three nights. (4) She yawned with her mouth wide
open, showing off her fillings. And (5) she ran with her limbs
akimbo, flailing in all directions when we were trying to make a
light—it was graceless and graceful all at once.

Oh, and (6) she snored.

She woke me up every night because of it. When I told her—on day three when I felt comfortable enough—she denied it. "That is a lie."

"Do I strike you as a liar?"

"*Non.* But in this instance, you lie."

The next night I recorded it on my phone from the alcove and played it back to her over breakfast.

"That is you," she said.

"How could it be me if I'm the one recording it?" I asked.

"You are playing a joke. That is you, pretending to be me."

The next night I talked softly over my recording so she would see it couldn't possibly be me. "See?" I said.

"It is Templeton. Bad Templeton." She shook her finger at him, then picked him up and rubbed his tummy while he purr-growled happily and grinned at her with his crooked teeth. "He *does* smile!" she exclaimed.

"Only with people he really likes."

Templeton adored Charlie. He loved to sit on her lap and stay there until his farts got too wicked and she put him back on the floor. If it weren't for his loyalty to me, I'm quite certain he'd have happily started a new life in France with her. (He would make a great French dog, because he walks with confidence and swagger. Plus he'd look spectacular in a dog-sized beret.)

We'd all fallen for Charlie. The Mumps took turns saying, "I wish we could adopt you!" Sal said she was "the bee's knees," which was his ultimate old-fashioned compliment.

He came to our house for dinner on Wednesday, like he always did. He'd brought a variety of patties from Lloyd's shop to "round out" the meal (code for making sure we had something edible if Mum was cooking).

"Where did you meet your wife?" Charlie asked him as we ate.

"At the Palais Royale. Beautiful old building on the Lake Shore. They held dances back then, and I literally swept her off her feet."

"When did she die? And how?" I marveled at her directness. I never asked Sal these questions; death-talk made me queasy.

"It's been three years, four months, and five days," he said. "Pancreatic cancer."

"I am very sorry for your loss. It sounds like you had a genuine romance."

"Oh, we did. We surely did."

After dinner the three of us went into the living room while the Mumps cleaned up. I took out a deck of cards and tried to teach Charlie how to play gin rummy—Sal and I played a lot of cards—but we didn't get very far, because Charlie and Sal were engrossed in conversation, this time all in French. I half listened, not understanding a word.

Till I heard *aquacise*.

"What are you guys talking about?"

"He is telling me about your Saturday mornings," said Charlie. "It sounds so fun!"

"I told her she should come," said Sal. "The ladies would love her."

"No!" I blurted. "I mean—sorry, but the class is full." The thought of Charlie seeing me in my red Speedo, with all of my six feet two inches worth of blindingly white flesh on display, made me want to pass out on the spot.

"I'm sure Carmen—" Sal began.

"Nope. It's out of her control. Fire regulations and all that. *Darn.* What a shame." I was eternally grateful that Mup was in the other room.

Sal gave me a penetrating look. But he let it drop. They went back to conversing in French, and I laid out a game of solitaire.

Bullet, dodged.

But I could not dodge Tyler Kertz.

He flirted with Charlie every chance he got.

On Thursday we went to the CN Tower. To get to the top, you have to ride in a *glass elevator* on the exterior of the tower. Who came up with that design? A cruel, heartless monster, that's who.

I tried. I really did. I got into the elevator. I faced the inner wall. I squeezed my eyes shut. Alex told me later that I made whimpering sounds even though we hadn't started moving yet. The elevator operator must have heard those sounds because he asked if I wanted off. I blurted, "Yes, oh please, yes!"

I scrambled out. The doors closed. Just before the elevator started its rapid ascent, I saw Tyler squeeze in beside Charlie, right at the front. He whispered something into her ear that made her laugh as they shot up fearlessly into the sky.

"That was a fail," Alex said afterward. "Tyler had her all to himself at the top of the world."

Fabrizio sidled up beside Alex. Under his jacket he was wearing a shirt with penguins all over it, and bright green pants. "What are you guys talking about?" Did I detect just a hint of uneasiness in his tone? Was it possible that my jealousy of his closeness with Alex worked both ways? "Is this about Wil's crush on Charlie?"

My eyebrows shot up. I looked at Alex. "You promised you wouldn't tell."

"I didn't, I swear."

"He didn't have to. I'm not blind."

Great. "Please don't say anything."

Fab pretended to zip his lips. "I won't. Besides, I think it's sweet. And not necessarily a fool's game."

"That's what I said." Alex smiled at Fab and grabbed his hand.

"What's on our agenda tomorrow?" asked Fab.

"The Royal Ontario Museum."

"That's your turf, Wil," said Alex. "You know that place inside out."

"There you go," said Fab. "Tomorrow, you don't leave her side. Be Charlie's personal tour guide."

But the next morning at the museum, Tyler clung to her like a leech.

I didn't know what to do. So I followed them. At one point I tried to steer Charlie toward the mummies, but he just moved right along with us.

I was feeling desperate, which is the only explanation I have for what I did next.

While Charlie read about the mummies, I tapped Tyler's arm. "Could I have a word?"

"Sure. Shoot."

"I am—"

"Oops, that's two words."

"Ha-ha, good one. I want to talk to you, man to man."

"Where's the second man?"

"Ha-ha. Um. I was just. I mean, the thing is. I like Charlie."

"Duh."

"And, I mean, I don't think you like her the way I do. So I was just wondering if you could maybe . . . back off a little?"

"Wait. You think I'm hitting on her?"

"Yes?"

"I have a girlfriend."

I let out a sigh of relief. "Really? Well, then, my apologies, I thought—"

"But she goes to boarding school, so. Out of sight, out of mind."

"So . . . you *are* hitting on her?"

He stared at me without blinking. "Let's see if I under-stand correctly. You think that if *I* back off, *you* might stand a chance."

I cleared my throat. "Maybe?"

"You think I'm your biggest obstacle?"

"I think that you are possibly a roadblock, yes."

He smiled sympathetically, and I thought for one fleeting mo-ment that I'd actually gotten through to him. "Oh, Wank. Poor, deluded Wank." He poked his finger into my soft belly. "You look like a life-sized Pillsbury Doughboy. You're *bland*. You're . . . nothing. You're . . . a zero. I'm not your biggest obstacle. *You* are your biggest obstacle." Then he walked back over to Charlie, who was still reading about the mummies.

I felt numb. I tugged at the sleeve of my sweatshirt. I could feel my eyes stinging. *Do not let him get to you!* I repeated the words in my head. I would not cry. I would *not*.

I left the Egyptian wing, and Charlie, and made a beeline for Fulton.

The foyer was fairly quiet. I lay down in between the metal slabs and stared up at Fulton's massive bones. Once upon a time, he'd roamed the Earth with his dinosaur buddies, until they were blasted into oblivion by a giant asteroid, an ice age, or both.

I tried to think of Sal's words. *In the history of the Earth, our lives are a blip!* In the scope of human existence, Tyler was right: I *was* nothing, but no more or less so than he was. In the scope of human existence, we were *both* blips.

These thoughts were oddly comforting. They calmed my mind and slowed my urge to burst into tears.

A shadow fell over me. "Wilbur?"

I shielded my eyes. "Mitzi?"

She looked down at me, her red hair held back by Hello Kitty barrettes. She wore black lace-up Doc Martens and overalls. "Why are you on the floor?"

"Just gaining perspective."

She nodded like this made sense. "Cool."

"What are you doing here?"

"Lame school trip." Mitzi went to an alternative school somewhere in Parkdale. "You?"

"Here with the French exchange students."

"How's that going?"

"Oh, you know. Fine."

A rare smile appeared on her face. "Hey, Franklin's perked up."

It took me a minute. "Glad to hear it."

"Well. See you soon, I guess."

"Yeah. See you."

She walked away. And I stayed where I was for a few minutes longer, until a group of kindergarten students wandered over and started giggling at the weirdo on the floor.

On Saturday morning I slipped out of bed and took Templeton for a quick walk before aquacise. Charlie and I had stayed up late with the Mumps the night before, playing an epic game of Qwirkle, and I figured she would relish the chance to sleep in.

I went next door to get Sal. He put on his fedora and grabbed his cane, and I helped him to the car. Mup had scraped the front windows and was ready to go. I eased Sal into the passenger seat and opened the back door.

"*Salut!*" said Charlie from the back seat.

"What are you doing here?" My voice rose an octave.

"She said she'd like to come, so I lent her a swimsuit," said Mup.

"Well, isn't this fantastic. Wilbur told us the class was full." Sal turned in his seat and gave me another one of his penetrating looks.

"What? Where did you get that from, Wil? There's plenty of room," Mup said oh-so-helpfully as she pulled away.

I didn't say a word during the entire drive. All I could think of was that Charlie was about to see the life-sized Pillsbury Doughboy.

In nothing but a bright red Speedo.

I was a mess in the change room. "I'm not feeling so good," I told Sal as he took off his rubber overshoes. "I think I'll just stay in my street clothes and watch from the sidelines."

Sal gave me a stern look. "I may be old, Wilbur, but I'm not stupid. Don't be that person."

"Which person is that?"

"The person who lets fear dictate his choices."

"Um, Sal? In case you haven't noticed, I have *always* been that person."

"Well, not today." He prodded me with his cane. "Get into your swimsuit. *Now.*"

"Ow! But I—"

"No buts. Do it!"

I opened my mouth to say no. Then I thought about little Salomon, who was orphaned at such a young age and had to get on a boat to England to start a whole new life.

And I started to get changed.

We headed out to the pool. I clutched my towel tightly around my body with my left hand while Sal held on to my right arm for support.

Ruth Gimbel and a few other women descended on Sal like vultures, circling him. "Sal, I baked homemade rugelach last night. I brought you a dozen," Ruth said. She was wearing her swim cap with the daisies all over it.

"*We* brought you homemade liverwurst," said Leah and Alice Johnson in unison. They were twin sisters in their late seventies. "I'm the younger one," Leah constantly reminded us. "By a full minute."

I sat on the bench, keeping my towel wrapped firmly around me like a cape.

Mup and Charlie stepped out of the women's change room.

Carmen is a foot shorter than Charlie and substantially wider, so the suit she'd loaned her was tight in some places and sagged in others. The cups in the chest area were comically big. One of them was dented.

And yet.

She still looked beautiful.

When Mup shouted, "Everyone into the pool!" I waited until Charlie jumped in. Only then did I drop my towel and jump in two rows behind her, so she wouldn't have a perfect, hour-long view of my jiggling white flesh.

Charlie was not a natural. It took her a long time to grasp the moves, and she did them all on the wrong side. If Mup started moving to the left, Charlie moved to the right. Ruth Gimbel was stationed beside her; they knocked into each other a bunch of times. Ruth started grumbling about "foreign interlopers." But Charlie didn't notice; she was having a great time.

My plan was to get out of the pool a few minutes before class ended. But then Mup played "Uptown Funk" and I got caught up in the music, and next thing I knew, class was over.

I panicked. I tried to wade through the water to the pool's edge, but Ethel Hiller—who's built like a tank and moves like a tortoise—blocked my way.

Suddenly Charlie was beside me. "That was so much fun!" She threw her arms around me and gave me a hug. When she released me, the second cup in her swimsuit was also dented, to match the first.

She had made contact with my pasty, pimply flesh. I was mortified on her behalf.

These were my decidedly unsexy thoughts when I felt Jeremiah stir.

I glanced down.

No.

No, no, no, no, no, no, no.

I used every ounce of willpower to think about boring things. I thought about erasers, but that made me think of the word *rubber,* which made me think of condoms. I thought about flowers, but that made me think about the Georgia O'Keeffe painting I'd seen at the AGO that looked like a vagina. I thought about volcanoes, because we'd been talking about Mount St. Helens in geography—eruptions; hot, flowing lava: bad!

"Time to get out, Wil, the next class is about to start," Mup yelled.

I stared into the mid-distance. I could feel my face heating up, even though the water was cold.

Almost everyone else had climbed out of the pool, except for Sal. "Come on, let's go," he said to me as he passed.

"I can't," I whispered.

"What do you mean—"

"I mean I can't!" I glanced down.

Sal followed my gaze. "Oh. Gotcha. Don't feel bad, kiddo. Happens to the best of us. Well—not to me anymore, not for years—"

"Come on you two, out of the pool!" Mup hollered from the deck.

Sal grabbed my arm. He made a loud groaning sound and doubled over in pain. "Agh!"

"You okay?" Mup asked.

"Bad leg cramp. Wilbur, stay with me till it passes."

"Of course." I gave him a grateful look. "Academy Award–winning performance."

He grinned. "Move over, Robert De Niro."

A minute or so later Jeremiah went back into hibernation, and the two of us got out of the pool.

Sal is the ultimate best friend.

Charlotte, my own spider
You have gotten in my head
Charlotte, my own spider
You have caught me in your web

From "Charlotte's Web" by Wilbur Nuñez-Knopf

THE FINAL FEW DAYS OF CHARLIE'S STAY WENT BY FAR too quickly.

"The last supper," Mum sighed as the five of us gathered around our small Formica table, because of course we'd invited Sal. Charlie looked beautiful in a multicolored muumuu, and I wore my nicest gray sweatshirt and jeans; we were going to a farewell dance at the school.

"We will really miss you," Mup said. "You're like our adopted daughter."

"I will miss you, too. You are my adopted mothers."

Templeton barked and barked as if he too understood she was leaving in the morning. Finally Charlie picked him up and put him on her lap, and even though he wasn't allowed at the supper table the Mumps let it slide just this once.

When we left for the dance, Sal held her hand in his and

raised it to his lips, just like he had when he'd first met her. "À bientôt," he said.

"That is perfect," she replied. "Not goodbye. Just until next time."

I was missing her already. Sal must have noticed, because he whispered to me as we left, "Relax, Wilbur. Stay in the moment. Try to have fun. Maybe you can use some of the dance moves I taught you!" Sal had tried to teach me and the Mumps the fox-trot on New Year's Eve, when we'd gathered to celebrate. I'd knocked over and broken Mum's favorite art deco lamp.

We picked up Alex, Fabrizio, and their billets on the way. The gym had been transformed; it was decorated with tons of glittery icicles and homemade paper snowflakes. We found a table to dump our coats onto. I was trying to gather up the courage to ask Charlie to dance, when she grabbed my hand and pulled me onto the dance floor.

She danced with such style! Sort of like the way she ran, with her limbs all over the place. I let myself go and tried to move like I did in the water at aquacise. For once in my life I didn't care if I looked like a dork.

Charlie and I danced for a long time. When the first slow song came on, she put her arms around my waist, and I did the same. She was tall enough to almost rest her head on my shoulder.

"I have had such a good time here, Wilbur. And it is all thanks to you."

"I feel the same way, my cherry."

She laughed. "Oh, Wilbur. It is not pronounced like the fruit. It is pronounced *sherEE.*"

"Oh."

She lifted her head. We gazed into each other's eyes. A jumble of thoughts crowded my brain. *Is this it? Is this my cue? Should I go in for a kiss?* But then other thoughts piled on top of my first thoughts: *Never assume a girl wants any kind of physical contact! Always ask first! (Mumps™).* Then I remembered that I'd never kissed a girl before, and what if I did it wrong? Maybe I should start by telling her how I felt about her; but how would I find the words? All of these thoughts fought for space in my head, and they were still fighting when the song ended, and she pulled away.

"Whew, I think I need a break," she said. We were both sweaty and hot. I poured her a glass of watery punch at the snack table, and she gulped it down. "I will be right back. I need to pee very badly." Then she added, *"Trop mignons, tes boutons!"*

And she kissed my cheek.

I was still touching the spot her lips had kissed, when Alex approached. He was wearing new jeans and a green polo shirt. "That color's good on you," I said. "Let me guess, Fabrizio took you shopping again?"

Alex nodded. "How's it going with Charlie?"

"Good," I said. "Really good. She just kissed my cheek. And she said something in French. Something about me. I caught *mignon* and *bouton.*"

"*Mignon* is 'cute.' . . . *Bouton* is 'button.' . . . Whoa. I think she said you're cute as a button!"

My heart leapt. "Really?"

Another slow song came on. And it wasn't just any song; it was "I Love You" by Billie Eilish. Fabrizio—who was dressed in a fire-engine red suit—grabbed Alex's hand. "Let's go."

Alex looked at me. "Find her. Ask her to dance. See how it goes. If it seems right . . . tell her how you feel. Maybe you'll get a kiss on the lips next time."

"Good luck!" added Fabrizio as he pulled Alex onto the dance floor. It was filling up with couples.

I scanned the room. I couldn't see Charlie.

I had another glass of punch and realized that I also needed to pee.

I left the gym and headed down the darkened corridor toward the washrooms.

I heard the noises first. Slurpy sounds, and little moans.

Then I saw them, down a side corridor, leaned up against the lockers, bodies intertwined.

"Mmmmmm," said the girl.

"Mmm-mmm," said the boy.

I quickened my pace.

Then something struck me.

The girl wore a multicolored muumuu.

I walked backward and peered down the corridor again.

And I forgot all about needing to pee.

* * *

"Charlie . . . and Tyler?" Alex asked moments later. He and Fabrizio had joined me at our table when the song was done. I sat, frozen, unable to move. "Are you sure?"

"Pretty sure. I mean, it was dark."

"This gym is a hotbed of hormones," said Fab. "It could have been anyone."

"He's right," said Alex, and for a moment I felt better.

"Hang on," said Fab. He dashed out of the gym. A few minutes later, he was back. His eyes were wide. "It was them, all right. Going at it, hot and heavy."

"Fab," said Alex.

"Sorry," said Fab. "Sorry, Wilbur." He sounded sincere.

"I didn't think she liked him *that* much," I said.

"She probably doesn't," said Fabrizio. "It's probably just one of those raw-animal-attraction-type things."

I groaned.

"Fab," said Alex again.

"I thought—" I began, but I stopped. What I was about to say was *so stupid and naïve.*

"You thought what?" asked Alex.

"I thought . . . that just maybe . . . she liked *me.*"

"Of course you did. I thought she did, too," said Alex.

"I mean, she kissed me," I continued. "On the cheek, but still. And she said I was cute as a button."

"*Cute* generally refers to babies. Or dogs. Or old people," said Fabrizio sympathetically.

"Fab," Alex said for the third time.

"What exactly did she say?" asked Fabrizio.

"She said, *trop mignons, tes boutons.*"

Fabrizio's eyebrows shot up. His mouth opened, then closed, like he was trying to figure out how to break the bad news. "Oh my. I'm so sorry, Wilbur. She said your zits were cute."

I wanted to go outside and lie down in a snowbank and fall asleep and never wake up.

We were all pretty quiet on the way home. Charlie walked ahead of us, chatting with Léo and Christophe in French. Alex and Fabrizio walked on either side of me, like they were afraid I might topple over at any moment.

When we got inside, Charlie went to the kitchen to get a glass of water but I went straight to bed, crawling onto my air mattress in the alcove without changing or brushing my teeth. Templeton is amazing at reading my emotions, and he knew I was upset. He made comforting little growls and curled his body closer to mine when I crawled into bed. "Thank you for always being there for me," I whispered to him. He gave me a soulful look. He licked my face. He farted.

But I held him close anyway and just breathed through my mouth.

A few minutes later Charlie came into the room. "That was a wonderful evening," she whispered.

For you, maybe, I thought.

"Thank you again, Wilbur. For everything." I heard her get into bed.

I knew I shouldn't ask. I *knew.* "Charlotte?" I said anyway, using her full name.

"Yes, Wilbur?"

"Why?"

"Why am I tired?"

"No. Why Tyler Kertz?"

"Oh my. Did somebody see us?"

I didn't tell her the somebody was me. "Yes."

She was quiet for a moment. "Well, he is handsome. He is, how do you say it? A *boy toy.*"

The metaphorical knife plunged into my heart. "But his personality . . ."

"Is not so good. He is a little bit boring and also very fond of himself. You are so much easier to talk to! But I didn't go with him to talk."

The knife plunged deeper.

There was silence for a while. I thought she'd gone to sleep. Then she said, "It has been so wonderful getting to know you, Wilbur."

For a split second, I felt just a tiny bit better. Then:

"You are like the younger brother I never had."

The knife went right through my heart and out the other side.

"Now if it is okay with you, your sister must sleep, and you must sleep, too." She yawned loudly. "Thank you, Wilbur. For everything. It has been a most magical trip."

I stared into the darkness. "Good night, Charlotte."

"Good night, Wilbur."

"Good night, Charlotte."

"Good night, Wilbur."

"Good night."

"Good night."

A few minutes later she started to snore like a trucker.

I've entered a black hole
And damaged my heart
Can't find the light switch
My world has gone dark

from "Black Hole" by Wilbur Nuñez-Knopf

AND THEN SHE WAS GONE.

Just four hours later, the Mumps drove Charlie to the school, where she boarded the bus with the other French students to go to the airport.

I stayed home. I said I was sick. Which wasn't totally a lie.

I lay in bed in the alcove all morning with Templeton. Turns out you can hear conversations in the kitchen really well from there.

"I think our Wil is suffering from a broken heart," Mum said when they got back from dropping off Charlie.

Mup: "He did moon over her like a puppy dog, didn't he?"

Mum: "Good goddess, yes."

Ouch. How dumb could I be, thinking my own mothers hadn't noticed?

Mum: "Not that I blame him. She's an amazing young woman, the type of girl he should be with."

Mup: "As opposed to all the other girls he's been with?"

Ouch squared.

Mum: "I just mean that when he does meet someone, I hope she's a little bit like Charlie."

Mup: "Me too. And he will. He's going to grow into an exceptional person and have great relationships with fabulous women."

Better.

Mup: "It just might take him three to five years longer than most people."

Aaaaaaagh!!!

I suddenly felt furious: with the Mumps, with Tyler, with Charlie, with the world—but mostly with myself.

So I did what any fourteen-year-old boy would do when he's full of rage.

I wrote a poem.

Black Hole

I've entered a black hole
And damaged my heart
Can't find the light switch
My world has gone dark

I fell in love
With a girl from Paris
My love was unrequited
And now I'm embarrassed

She saw me as a good friend
A brother, at best
And not like Cersei and Jaime Lannister
We're not talking incest

Nor like Dany Targaryen and Jon Snow
Wow. Game of Thrones *was*
Incest-heavy
For one TV show

I've entered a black hole
And damaged my heart
Can't find the light switch
My world has gone dark

I stayed home all day. The next morning, Friday, Mup came into my room, dressed in the one-piece coverall she used at the doggie daycare. I'd transferred out of the alcove and back into my own bed. "Wilbur, you need to go to school."

"Please. I can't."

"Look at me." I rolled over to face her. "Darling, you need to get back on the horse—" She stopped. She took in my blotchy face and red eyes. Her tone softened. To my surprise, she said, "Okay. You can miss one more day. But that's it. You don't want your grades to suffer." My grades were mediocre at the best of times. She smoothed my hair and kissed my cheek. "I'll make you your favorite dish for dinner tonight, okay?"

"Really? Spaghetti with—"

"Butter and salt."

"Yum."

"Love you, my boy." She got up to leave.

"Mup?"

"Yes, my darling?"

"Have you ever had your heart broken?"

"Oh, goodness, yes. Many times. It's horrible. But it does get better. I know it might be hard to believe right now, but it won't feel like this forever."

Then she sat back down and scratched my back like she used to when I was little, and I drifted back to sleep.

By Saturday morning, Mup's stores of sympathy were used up. At eight thirty she marched into my room in the blue tracksuit that she wore over her bathing suit and yanked off the covers. "I don't expect you to come to aquacise. But I do expect you to get up and walk your dog, because neither Mum nor I have time to do it, and he's your responsibility. And lastly, if I'm not mistaken, you have a shift at Foot Long today, and it's far too late for you to call in sick."

She waited for me to crawl out of bed. When I moved past her to go to the washroom, she waved a hand in front of her face. "Whew! You smell like rotten brussels sprouts and foot fungus. Shower!"

I checked my phone while I pooped. Alex had texted me a bunch of times, wondering where I was. It was nice that he'd noticed, but I hadn't had the energy to text back.

Mup had already left when I got downstairs, but Mum was drinking coffee at the kitchen table, still in her floral kimono, reading from a script. The moment I walked in she stood and enveloped me in a hug. "How are you doing, peanut?"

I shrugged. I could feel the tears coming; she was my Mum, after all.

"Sweet boy." She hugged me for a long time. Eventually I broke free and blew my nose on a wadded-up tissue I found in my pocket. I poured kibble into Templeton's bowl and popped some bread into the toaster. "Do you have an audition?" I asked.

"Yes. On Monday. Will you run my lines with me?"

"Of course."

She handed me the pages. "You're the lead. Joseph. The scene takes place in a doctor's reception area. Joseph is talking to someone on the phone."

"'Look, Marianne,'" I read, "'we've been through this a thousand times, I can't pick up the kids on Thursdays. I have my AA meeting and you know how important it is that I go—'"

"'Excuse me? The doctor will see you now,'" Mum, or "Receptionist," said.

I flipped to the next page, but it was a new scene. "That's it?"

"Yup. But did you notice, in my delivery I have a hint of disapproval in my voice; like, 'He's talking loud on his phone in a quiet waiting room?' I'm hoping that might give me an edge."

"Sounds like an excellent plan."

After breakfast I took Templeton for a walk. He was in a sassy mood and barked at the bigger dogs, including a huge Bernese mountain dog, who cowered behind his owner. We stopped at Stoner Park, and I threw a ball for him. He ran back and forth in front of Lloyd and Viktor, who sat on their usual bench. At one point Templeton didn't come back with the ball; he rooted around in a corner of the park instead. "Wilbur," said Lloyd. "Your dog is eating another dog's poo."

Templeton ignored my whistles, and I finally had to march over and pick him up. He immediately started licking my cheek. Lloyd and Viktor gagged in horror. "Dude!" shouted Viktor.

I gave my face another good scrub when I got home.

I was scheduled to open today, so shortly before eleven I forced myself to walk down to Foot Long. I pride myself on being a reliable person, and also now that I was a Submarine Sandwich Creation Expert, I felt a certain weight of responsibility. I repeated one of Mup's sayings in my head: *The show must go on.*

Mitzi was at the door, shivering in her peacoat, when I arrived. I let us both in with my key. "Wow am I happy you're back," she said. "Dmitry is such a dick."

"He's still a dick when I'm here."

"Yeah, but your presence dilutes the overall dick vibe." We both disappeared into the back and reemerged in our yellow polyester pit-stop outfits. Like superheroes. Only not. *So* not. The overhead fluorescent lights buzzed unpleasantly, so I put on the store Muzak.

"Speaking of Dmitry," I said, "wasn't he supposed to be here by now?"

"Yep."

The two of us prepped, enjoying the lull before the lunch rush. "Wow, a Muzak version of 'Good as Hell,'" she said. "It's oddly catchy."

"I would have to agree."

"How was your week with the French students?" she asked as she refilled the jalapeño bin.

I laid out cheese slices, thinking about how to respond. "Mostly fun." It had been like a Dickens novel: the best of times; the worst of times.

"You get to go visit them too, right? In Paris?"

"Yeah. Except I don't think I'm going to go."

"Why not?"

I told her half of the truth. "It's a lot of money. I don't think I can get it together in time."

"I hear you. I'm trying to save money for a trip this summer."

"Where to?"

"Missouri. This year's setting for the Pennsic Wars."

"The what?"

"Have you heard of the Society for Creative Anachronism?"

"I have not."

"We're a living history group. We dress up in costumes and re-create medieval history. Mostly battles. The Pennsic War is a made-up battle between different groups of anachronists."

I looked at her more closely. "Wow. That . . . is . . ."

"Weird, I know. But it's a ton of fun." She lifted her armpit and inhaled her own scent. "Ugh, this jumpsuit stinks like boiled cabbage no matter how often I wash it."

Dmitry finally strolled in, a full half hour late. He was wearing baggy jeans that rode way down his butt and a puffy jacket. His headphones leaked loud music. "You're late," I said, stating the obvious.

He just kept moving to the beat, his jeans dropping even lower.

"YOU'RE LATE."

Nothing.

I grabbed his headphones. *"YOU'RE LATE!"*

He swatted my hand away. "No need to shout, Winston." He slipped them around his neck.

"Wilbur. Get into your uniform. And do the bathroom check while you're back there."

"Look, Wellington—"

"*Wilbur.* You know my name is Wilbur—"

"You've forgotten about my condition. My psoriafungalitis."

"I know that's a crock."

"It is not," he said, looking wounded.

"It so is," said Mitzi.

"You don't believe me, I'll get a note from my doctor. Maybe I'm mispronouncing it or something."

The door opened and a large group came in, ready to order. I didn't want them to see me argue with an employee, so I caved. "Fine. Bring a note from your doctor next time. Just—hurry and get changed, we're about to get busy."

He did not hurry.

He sauntered.

I glanced at Mitzi and caught her disappointed look.

All my bad feelings came flooding back. Tyler's words echoed in my head. *You're nothing. You're a zero.*

How could I have thought for one nanosecond that a girl like Charlie would ever be interested in a guy like me?

I wasn't interested in a guy like me.

I'd forgotten my phone at home, and when I got back, I had a few more text messages from Alex and a handful from Sal. His texts were full of bizarre autocorrects.

I missed you at acquaintance.

Why weren't you at the poop?

Come for lunch? I'll make grilled Jesus.

Sorry your fart is broken.

You will still have fur in parasites.

110

I'm ashamed to admit that I still didn't respond, to either of them.

On Sunday night, Sal didn't come for dinner because he had some big pinochle tournament in London, Ontario. After I'd crawled into bed with Templeton, I finally sent Sal and Alex a joint response to their texts.

Thx for your messages. I'm OK. I am not going to Paris. Pls don't try to change my mind.

Then I put my phone on Do Not Disturb and fell into a fitful sleep.

My heart, it is wounded
My heart, it hurts
I want to punch my nemesis
Tyler Kertz

From "Aches & Pains" by Wilbur Nuñez-Knopf

BY MONDAY MORNING, THE MUMPS HAD DRIVEN STRAIGHT past Sympathy and right into Tough Love. "You are not staying home again," Mup said over breakfast. "You know what they say. You've got to get back on the horse that bucked you."

"Your horse analogies are lost on me," I replied. "For one thing, I've never been *on* a horse. They're huge. They're terrifying—"

Mup slammed her fist on the table. Our bowls of porridge jumped. "If I have to drive stressed-out people in gridlocked downtown traffic all day and your mum has to be a background actor in an adult-diaper ad, you can bloody well pull yourself together and get your butt to school!"

Unlike the horse analogy, I had to concede that this made some sense.

* * *

112

So I went to school. I got through the day. Tyler wasn't in any of my Monday classes, which was a small mercy. Whenever I spotted him in the halls with his basketball friends, I turned and walked the other way.

But there was no avoiding him at band practice after school. Every time he caught my eye, he made rude gestures, most of which involved thrusting his pelvis, honking imaginary breasts, and waggling his tongue. I dreaded the end of practice. But fifteen minutes before we finished, Tyler left for a swim meet.

"Thank you all for being such good hosts to our French counterparts," Mr. P said when practice was officially over. "If you're like me, you must be missing them terribly." His voice actually trembled; then he pasted on a brave smile. "But fear not—we will see them in two short months! And remember to bring in your checks for the remainder as soon as you can."

I would not be bringing in a check. But I didn't need to tell Mr. P that yet.

I was still packing up my instruments when I saw Alex and Fabrizio leave the band room together without a backward glance.

Even though they were joined at the hip, they usually waited for me. Given everything else that had happened—and given that Alex and Fab both *knew* what had happened—it felt like a whole lot of salt poured into an already gaping wound.

* * *

The Mumps were still at work when I got home. Templeton, however, was very much there, and he went wild with happiness when he saw me. His long body wound its way through my legs in little figure eights. He was a ray of sunshine on a crap day. I picked him up and his little tail went *thwap thwap thwap* against my arm. "At least *you* love me, Templeton." He gave me a snaggletoothed grin.

I knocked three times on Sal's wall and waited.

And waited.

I knocked again, three times. Still no answer.

He's probably angry with me, too, I thought. But at the same time, I felt a worm of fear.

I pulled out my phone and called his number. It rang and rang.

It's nothing. He just doesn't want to talk to me.

But how could I know for sure?

I grabbed Sal's spare key from a hook in the hallway. With Templeton tucked under my arm like a football, I headed next door.

I rang the bell. No answer. "Sal?" Nothing. I let myself in. I could hear a low hum. "Sal?"

I hurried to his kitchen. It was empty. I was about to run upstairs when I saw him, sitting in the living room.

He was in his favorite wingback chair, in his plaid sweater and black pants, his favorite fuzzy pink slippers on his feet. The humming grew louder.

"Sal!" I put Templeton down and hurried over to him. His eyes were open. I put my hand on his neck to check his pulse.

He swatted my hand away. "What the hell are you doing?"

"I thought you were—"

"I'm not dead. I'm fed up."

"With what?"

"With *you*. And I'm not the only one."

"Hello, Wilbur," said a familiar voice behind me.

I turned. Alex sat on the couch. The humming was coming from him. Fabrizio sat next to him.

I was utterly confused. "What's going on?"

"You texted us both on the weekend," Alex said. "So Sal had my contact info. He called me this morning to talk about you."

"But—why?"

"Because enough is enough," Sal replied. "Wilbur Nuñez-Knopf: welcome to your intervention."

They said you need an intervention
Not for booze, or crack, or E
Had nothing to do with the usual addictions
It was about saving me, from me

From "Intervention" by Wilbur Nuñez-Knopf

"SIT," SAID SAL, HIS TONE STERN. HE POINTED TO A straight-backed wooden chair that had been placed in the middle of the Persian carpet, strategically positioned to face the three of them.

"Wait, I don't get it—"

"SIT."

Templeton and I both sat, me on the chair, Templeton at my feet. One of us started licking his nonexistent nuts.

"I called Alex this morning because I was worried. Turns out he was worried, too."

"How many texts have I sent you over the past few days?" asked Alex.

"A lot?"

"And how many did you respond to?"

"Um. One?"

"Not cool, Wil, not cool. We're friends, and friends don't do that to each other."

Okay, I'll admit it: I enjoyed hearing him use the word *friends* twice in one sentence. "Sorry. I'm sorry. I've just—" I could feel my eyes welling up, and it was hard to swallow. "I've been having a rough time."

Sal's tone softened. "I get it, kid. Unrequited love can be a real arse-kick."

"But it doesn't mean you shouldn't go to Paris!" Alex blurted.

"Exactly," said Sal.

"I can't. It would kill me."

Fabrizio sighed. "It wouldn't *actually* kill you."

"It might. I could get so distraught seeing Charlie and Tyler together, I might fall into the Seine and get swept away. Or step off the sidewalk and get hit by a tour bus—"

"*Dios mío.*" He exhaled loudly again and crossed his legs, which were clad in bright red pleather pants.

"If it's any consolation," Alex said, "I thought she liked you, too."

"Oh, she liked me, all right. *Like a brother.* Also, she told me I looked like a guy from an old movie. Napoleon Dynamite. Which I thought was a good thing until yesterday I looked him up."

"I know it's painful right now, Wilbur," said Sal. "But you'll get over Charlie. No doubt she is a very special girl, but there are plenty of fish in the sea."

"Not in the sea of high school, Sal. Not for me. I have too

much baggage. Besides, with my luck, the only fish I'd attract is the candiru."

"What's the candiru?"

"A fish that enters the human penis and eats it from the inside."

Alex squeezed his legs together. "Gaaaaaah!"

"Why did you tell us that?" said Fab. "Now I'll have the picture forever and always seared in my brain!"

"Sorry." But I wasn't.

"Wilbur," said Sal, trying to get us back on track. "Set aside Charlie for a moment. It's *Paris*. There's a lot more to this trip than a girl."

"He's right," said Alex.

"Easy for you guys to say. Sal, every time you went to the City of Love, you went with Irma. And you two"—I indicated Alex and Fab—"will be going on the trip together."

"But if we broke up tomorrow, I would still go," said Alex.

Fabrizio looked at him. "You would?"

Alex thought about it for a moment. "Yes. I would. Wouldn't you?"

Fabrizio thought about it, too. "Yes. I'd keep my distance from you, and I'd probably say horrible things about you behind your back . . . but I'd still go."

"But then what if one of you started seeing some hot French guy?" I asked.

"I would be miserable," Alex conceded. "But at least I would be miserable *in Paris*. I would drown my sorrows in delicious

French food. I would stuff myself with cassoulet and coq au vin." His eyes widened just thinking about it. "I would take a cooking course at the Cordon Bleu school!"

"I would sit in a café and drink absinthe and listen to Edith Piaf singing *'Non, je ne regrette rien'* while gazing dolefully at the chic Parisians passing by," Fabrizio continued. "My heartbreak would have so much *atmosphere*." They both stared into the distance, picturing their separate post-breakup Parisian scenes.

"What makes you so sure Charlie will get together with this Tyler kid, anyway?" asked Sal.

"Because they got together here."

"So? Alex told me it was more of a—what did you call it, Alex?"

"A hookup," said Alex. "And there's no guarantee it'll happen again."

"Very true," said Fab.

"There's no guarantee that it won't," I replied.

Sal crossed his arms over his chest. "Boy, oh boy. You're just rolling into a ball like a doodlebug and giving up, aren't you?"

"What choice do I have?"

"We always have choices, Wilbur. You can't force someone to like you, but you can at least *try*." Sal leaned forward in his chair. "When I met Irma at the Palais Royale, she was dating a blond Adonis from a wealthy family. All I had was my funny-looking face and a job at someone else's furniture store."

"You don't have a funny-looking face," I said. A white lie.

"Let me finish. We had a swell time dancing that night, so she agreed to let me take her to lunch one day the following week. I picked her up from her office job and took her to Fran's. We enjoyed our conversation. So we started going once a week. She got to know me as a person. And she realized she felt a lot more for me than she did for Mr. Adonis. She broke up with him, and a year later, we were married. Her parents never accepted me, but we didn't care."

"What a beautiful story," said Fabrizio.

"Didn't I say that, Wil?" said Alex. "Didn't I say women love character?"

"But I don't *have* character."

"Of course you do," said Sal.

I shook my head. "No. I don't. I'm not a lover *or* a fighter. I'm not you, Sal."

"Well, then, who are you?" asked Sal. "Who do *you* think you are?"

A wave of emotion crashed over me. "A loser. A nothing. A zero!"

Sal's old-man watery eyes suddenly looked extra watery. "Really? That's how you see yourself?"

And it was like I was ten again and watching the Sarah McLachlan SPCA ad, because I burst into tears.

Talk about humiliating. The room went deathly quiet. The only sound was the ticking of the grandfather clock in Sal's hallway.

Then Templeton started to howl, upset that I was upset.

I picked him up and put him on my lap. He started licking my tears.

"That's the same tongue that was just burrowing in his crotch—" Fabrizio started, but Alex squeezed his leg to stop him.

Sal got up from his chair and came over to me. "Wilbur, if you don't like yourself, this is truly a sad state of affairs." He patted my shoulder. "*We* like you. Right, boys?"

"Definitely," said Alex.

Fab cleared his throat. "I like Wilbur just as much as Wilbur likes me."

"We clearly see a better version of you than you do yourself," said Sal. "But I can tell you over and over again what a great kid you are; if you don't feel it yourself, it's meaningless. Charlie, Paris . . . all of it is meaningless."

"Somehow we have to get *you* to like you," said Alex.

Fabrizio snorted. "If *I* can learn to like *myself*? Anyone can."

It was my turn to snort. "What? You're one of the most"— I was going to say *arrogant*—"confident people I've ever met. You like yourself just fine." *Maybe too much.*

"I did like myself. Till I was about ten. Then I spent the last few years feeling the exact opposite." Fabrizio's voice cracked just a little, and Alex grabbed his hand. "Try coming out at age eleven at an all-boys' Catholic school. Some of the teachers were the worst. Even though I know for a fact at least two of them were also gay. Pretty hard to like yourself when everyone else is telling you you're an aberration."

"You boys are breaking my heart," said Sal.

My heart wasn't breaking. My heart was being kind of a dick. *This is supposed to be about* me. *And somehow he's made it about him.* I am not proud that those were my thoughts.

"It's okay, Sal," Fabrizio continued. "I worked at it. Really hard. Getting out of that school helped a lot. And now . . . I think I'm pretty great, just the way I am."

Alex kissed his cheek. "You are! You are perfection!"

"I wholeheartedly agree," said Sal, even though he barely knew Fab.

"But with Wilbur, we don't have the luxury of time. We barely have two months," said Fab.

We sat in silence for a while. *It's impossible,* I thought.

Then Fabrizio slapped a hand over his mouth. "Oh!"

"What?"

"I quite possibly have a genius idea." He paused for dramatic effect, which, given that his dad runs a dinner theater and he's sometimes recruited to stand in for a sick actor, is something he is very good at. "We do a *Queer Eye.*"

"Huh?"

But Alex was already nodding. "Yes!" He started to laugh his infectious laugh, and soon the rest of us had joined in, even though two of us had no idea why.

"What's a queer eye?" asked Sal.

"It's a makeover show on TV," said Alex. "In one of the iterations, five gay men give a complete lifestyle and attitude overhaul to a straight guy—"

"And simultaneously stamp out fear and ignorance and spread love and understanding, one hetero at a time," added Fabrizio.

"Sounds amazing," said Sal.

"And they do it in a really short period of time. The team is always trying to prepare their subject for some big upcoming event, like a party or a presentation." Fabrizio looked at me. "Your event is Paris!"

I just stared at them, trying to play catch-up in my head.

"Count me in," said Sal. "Wilbur? What do you say?"

I thought about it for a moment. "I don't know. I guess?"

"Let's hug it out," said Alex. We all stood and embraced, which was nice because the Mumps and I believe that men should be more in touch with their emotions in general. We pulled apart and Alex and I did our special handshake. I have to admit that for a moment I felt a bit hopeful again.

Then Fabrizio pursed his lips and looked me up and down. "We've set ourselves a difficult—nay, perhaps impossible—task. We have *a lot* of work to do."

"And only eight weeks to do it," said Alex.

"*Oy vey*," said Sal.

Which took away some of my good feelings, I will admit.

MAKEOVER

BELIEVE

"I LOVE YOU. I LOVE YOU. I LOVE YOU." I STARED AT MYself in the bathroom mirror exactly forty-eight hours later, wearing nothing but my underwear, which were old and gray and saggy. I tried to smile, but it was more like a grimace; it was impossible not to notice the enormous whitehead in the crease of my nose. So I popped it. Some of the goop hit the mirror, so I cleaned it off before I tried again.

"I love you. You are an incredible person. You are a winner!"

A sallow-skinned flabby weakling with moobs and a potbelly stared back at me.

He looked extremely skeptical.

The four of us—"The Fab Four," Fabrizio dubbed us, which in my opinion was remarkably self-serving—had reconvened after school at Sal's place the day before. They'd made me stand in the middle of the living room while they circled around me, like I was a statue on display at a museum. They critiqued me like I was a statue, too—an inanimate object that couldn't hear *every single word* they were saying.

Fabrizio: "His height is an advantage. But his hair looks like an out-of-control Chia Pet."

Alex: "He has terrible posture. It doesn't help with his overall physique."

I gave Sal a beseeching look, and he spoke up. "He's got no class, no style. He looks like a schlub."

Me: "Might I remind you all, *I can hear you.* And also, I feel there's an undertone of body-shaming going on here."

Fabrizio: "Not true. I'm fat—"

Alex: "Me, too—"

Me: "See, I would use words like *stocky,* or *powerfully built*—"

Fabrizio: "Thank you. But my point is that you can be any shape or size. You just have to know how to rock it." He swept his hands down his body; he was wearing a shirt with lemurs all over it, and his bright green pants. "*I* know how to rock it."

Sal bent down to give Templeton a belly rub. I heard his knees crack. "Fellas, I think we're getting ahead of ourselves. None of this outward appearance stuff is going to matter if we don't work on Wilbur's insides."

"Are you saying there's something wrong with my *insides,* too?"

"You have many outstanding qualities," said Sal. "You're kind, thoughtful, generous—an excellent friend. And you've got real promise as a writer."

"Very true," said Alex. "We've even turned some of his poems into songs."

"You have?" asked Fabrizio, with just the hint of a pout.

"Yes, and they're not half-bad."

I stood a little taller.

"You have a lot of great features," said Alex. "We just have to figure out how to draw those out and try to help you improve on the . . . less great ones."

"Number one, you are woefully lacking in self-confidence," said Sal.

"Even the way you walk," said Fabrizio. "It's like you're trying to make yourself smaller."

"And you always try to fade into the background," said Alex.

"So true!" said Fab. "Half the time I forget you're even there!"

"Aaaaagh!" I collapsed onto Sal's couch, head in my hands.

"Don't fret," said Fab. "I brought help." He picked up his Herschel school bag and dumped the contents onto the floor. "I thought these could spark ideas." They were books with titles like *The Blueprint: How to Be a Better You, Learning to Love Yourself,* and *"I Should've Had the Jalapeño Chicken Sandwich"—How to Live Life Without a Million Small Regrets.*

"Where did you get all of these?" asked Sal.

"My dad ordered tons of self-help books when my stepmom

left. We were two guys feeling lousy about ourselves for different reasons. So he'd finish one and pass it on to me, and vice versa. We even highlighted a bunch of stuff."

Sal bent down again and picked up some of the books. "Keep in mind, we need to tackle this in bite-sized pieces. Otherwise it's going to feel overwhelming, for Wilbur and for us. We want to set him up for success, not failure."

"That makes sense," said Alex as Sal handed each of us a book.

"Okay," he said. "Start reading."

That's how I came to stand in front of the bathroom mirror, repeating the same words over and over. Alex had found the idea in a book called *Self-Esteem in Six Simple Steps!* "The book says that if you repeat your mantra every day for at least five minutes, you'll start to believe it."

So I tried again, with more feeling. "I love you. You are an incredible person. You are a WINNER!"

"Did you say something, pickle?" Mum shouted from down the hall. "You need a fresh roll of TP?"

"No, I'm good!"

I said the next few rounds in a quieter voice.

And crazy as it sounds, by the time I was done with my five minutes, I could almost believe I *was* a winner.

Well.

Maybe not a winner. But just a tiny bit less of a loser.

FAKE IT TILL YOU MAKE IT

SAL WAS STANDING ON HIS PORCH, BUNDLED UP IN A thick wool sweater, when I stepped outside to go to school. It was way too cold to be outside; I was pretty sure he was simply waiting to see me. "Remember, Wilbur," he said. "Stand up straight. Be proud of your height. Hold your head high. Look people in the eye. Smile!" Then he added his own special *Charlotte's Web* message to me: "You're terrific! Radiant! Some pig!"

I gave my best friend a hug. "Thanks, Sal. You're all those things, too." He waved goodbye as I started my next assignment: the long solo walk to school.

They'd told me I had to walk alone for at least a week. And I wasn't allowed to keep my head down. I had to walk with confidence. My insides quivered, because Torontonians generally don't like it when people look them in the eye. It's not that

131

they're less friendly than other Canadians; they've just learned strategies to avoid weird encounters, which happen more often when you live in a big city. I still remember when we first moved here, a friendly-looking man smiled at me on the street, and when I smiled back, he opened his raincoat to reveal that aside from shoes and socks, he was totally naked underneath. Personally, I can't imagine anything more humiliating than having random strangers see Jeremiah at his softest and tiniest, but this guy seemed to take pride in it.

So walking with my head held high and looking people in the eye took some serious effort. "Remember, you don't have to *feel* confidence," Fabrizio had said to me the day before. "You just have to *project* confidence. It's what I did for ages. It's what I still do once in a while. Fake it till you make it!"

For the most part it went okay, except for one very big guy with a neck tattoo who glared at me and said, "What are you looking at, muppet?"

I was relieved when I arrived at school. Alex and Fabrizio were waiting for me by my locker; whether they'd intended it or not they were in matching color schemes, purple on top, black on bottom.

"Did you practice your mantra this morning?" asked Alex.

"I did. And I can't believe I'm saying this, but I feel like it made a tiny difference." I took off my coat and hung it up, waiting for them to congratulate me.

Instead Fabrizio took in my outfit and shook his head. "How can one person own so much beige?"

"Baby steps, Fabrizio, remember?" said Alex. Suddenly he covered his nose. "Ugh, what's that smell?"

It turns out holding your head high comes with certain risks.

I spent the next fifteen minutes in the washroom, using a stick to dig dog poop out of the treads of my boots.

But crazy as it sounds, I *did* feel small improvements over the week. The repetition of my tasks made a difference. I felt a little less blue. In phys ed I felt like I ran around the track faster than I ever had before, even though I only came in ahead of Peter Jensen, and he currently has to wear a leg brace. In English class I actually raised my hand to answer a question.

I felt just a tiny bit better about *me*.

Until I saw Tyler, and my new confidence spontaneously combusted into a tiny heap of beige-colored ashes.

He was in fine form after our next band practice. The basketball team had won the city championships the day before, which had wound him up big-time. He snuck up on Jo Lin and blasted his sax loudly; she almost burst into tears. He marched up to Alex and Fab and said, "You two are so cute together. Chubby and Chubbier." Alex immediately started to hum and blink. Even Fab looked upset. "You're an asshat, Kertz."

"Relax! Jeez, learn to take a joke, people. Seriously, I don't care if you guys make fun of me. Go for it! It's all in fun!"

"It's not fun if no one else is laughing," said Laura.

"Oh, Lucas, relax," he said, then "remembering": "I mean, Laura."

It was my turn next. "Hey, Wank. No hard feelings, eh?"

"I'm sure I don't know what you're talking about."

"Right. Okay." I finished packing up my instruments. "You do know you never stood a chance, right? Charlie's, like, a seven—"

I snapped to attention. "A seven? Are you out of your mind? She's an *eleventy-seven*—"

"In your universe, maybe. My point is—you've got to lower the bar. Find someone at your level. Like a troll, living under a bridge." He laughed. When I didn't join in he said, "Kidding! Man, what is with everyone today? Sense of humor much?"

Then he did something truly awful before he walked away.

He patted my arm.

His "humor" was bad enough.

His pity was worse.

LESS IS MORE

ON FRIDAY I SAT WITH ALEX AND FAB IN A CORNER OF the cafeteria. They were eating fries with gravy. I was trying to digest the quinoa fritters Mum had made the night before. My phone pinged.

It was a text from Charlie; our first communication since she'd gone home.

> Bonjour Wilbur! Sorry I have not texted sooner! It has been very busy since I got back with much homework to catch up on. How R U?

Alex read her text over my shoulder. I started to type a response. "What are you saying?"

"Not much."

> Things aren't the same without you here. I miss you terribly and—

Alex slapped the phone from my hand. It landed on the table. Fabrizio picked it up and read. His eyes widened. "Assassin! You are your own assassin!" He deleted my message and started typing.

"What are you—"

"Saving you from yourself."

I tried to grab my phone, but Alex stopped me. "Let him do his thing, Wil. He is a master."

Fab showed me what he'd typed.

Great.

"That's it?" I asked. He pressed Send. A moment later he pointed to the screen. Three moving dots; she was typing a response.

I am home, but I am homesick! I miss you and my new mothers very much.

"Can I have my phone back?"

"No."

"But I should respond—"

"No, you should not."

"But—that's rude."

Alex shook his head. "No. It's strategic." He held out his hand, and Fab gave him my phone. Alex tucked it into his backpack.

"What are you—you can't—"

"I'm keeping it till the end of the day."

"Then you're allowed to send Charlie a smile emoji," said Fab.

"That's it?"

"That's it."

"But—that says nothing—"

"Oh, Wilbur. Oh, young grasshopper," said Fab as he popped one of my quinoa fritters into his mouth, then made a face and spat it out. "Sit at my feet and learn from a master. A smile emoji, sent hours after her text, says, *I'm busy enjoying a rich and full life. I barely have time to respond to you. But you are someone I care about, therefore I don't want to NOT respond, so I send this emoji because it's fast and simple and you can read absolutely nothing into it.*"

I stared at him. "One smile emoji says all that?"

"Yep."

Alex beamed at Fabrizio. "He sent me *so many* smile emojis when we started dating."

Fabrizio reached across the table and took Alex's hand. "I was reeling you in a little bit at a time."

At the end of the school day, as promised, Alex gave me back my phone. I selected a smiley-face emoji to send to Charlie.

But just before I pressed Send, Alex grabbed the phone away from me again and showed it to Fabrizio.

"Not the one with the hearts for eyes! *Dios mío,* it's like trying to teach a giraffe to sing!"

Alex held the phone out of my reach. "I need you to promise me something before I give this back to you. Any time you want to text Charlie, you have to let me vet it."

"That's ridiculous." I reached for my phone—

Alex slipped it down the front of his pants.

"Please tell me it's between your jeans and your undies."

"Nope. Skin on skin." He started to laugh, and as per usual it was so infectious, I almost started laughing too, till I remembered where my phone was. "It stays there till you promise." When I didn't answer right away, he started gyrating his hips. "Oops. It's slipping down toward my oysters—"

"Aaaaagh! Fine. I promise."

He fished out my phone. He selected the blandest smiley-face emoji of them all and pressed Send. Then he dug around in his backpack, found a wet wipe, and gave my phone a thorough clean.

Alex is considerate that way.

USE YOUR WORDS

I WAS SO FOCUSED ON MY SELF-IMPROVEMENT PLAN that I'd conveniently forgotten about the more practical obstacle that stood in the way of me and Paris:

Money.

On Thursday after school, Mr. Papadopoulos asked to speak with me. He leaned against a kettledrum, sporting a black turtleneck and brand-new, stiff, dark blue jeans. "Wilbur." He stroked his chin. He had the beginnings of what I think was supposed to be a goatee but looked more like a tuft of belly button fluff. "I was going through my records last night. I still haven't received the rest of your money for our trip. Twelve hundred dollars."

"Sorry, sir."

"I'll need it at least two weeks ahead."

"Yes, sir."

"It would be a real shame if you couldn't go."

I was touched by the compliment. "Thank you, sir. I do think my triangle, tambourine, and cowbell add a certain *pop* to our music—"

"I—no. I just meant that the flights are booked and paid for. You won't get your deposit back."

"Oh. I can bring in what I've saved from my part-time job. I have at least one hundred and twenty dollars. . . ."

"That's one tenth of what you owe," he pointed out, not unkindly. "Just—talk to your mothers. Maybe we can come up with some sort of installment plan between now and then? I would still need full payment before we leave."

"Okay, Mr. P. Thank you."

He walked me to the door. "Since you're here, I'm gathering opinions."

"On what?"

"I'm trying a new look for—for Paris." His skin, I noticed, had turned a bright shade of pink.

"Ah."

He stroked the dust bunny on his chin. "Keep? Or lose?"

"Um. I would vote for lose?"

His face fell. "Really?" He glanced at me, in my beige sweatshirt and baggy beige pants, and his expression brightened. "But fashion isn't really your thing, is it?"

"Definitely not."

"Meaning I can take your opinion with a grain of salt?"

"Absolutely, Mr. P. It's what most people do."

* * *

That evening when I took Templeton out for his post-dinner walk, we wandered past Lloyd's patty shop; he was just locking up for the night. "Hey, Wilbur. Hang on." He went back into the shop and returned with two paper bags. "These ones are vegetarian, for your mothers. These ones are beef, for Sal. Just a few that didn't get sold today."

"Thanks, Lloyd." Lloyd knew that we, and Sal, were on tight budgets.

"And this one's for your ugly dog." He tossed a misshapen beef patty to Templeton, who barked his thanks before gobbling it up.

When I got home, I took off my boots and Templeton's booties and headed into the kitchen, ready to broach the subject of money with the Mumps.

Their heads were bent over Mup's laptop. "I don't know how we're short again. It feels like every month, we're short," she said.

"It's the unforeseen stuff. The leak in the roof . . . another mouth to feed for ten days . . ."

"That entirely avoidable parking ticket . . ."

"Don't rub it in, love."

Mup gave Mum a kiss. "But it's so much fun, Dove." She pushed her curls out of her face and sighed. "We've already missed a mortgage payment. We can't miss another one."

"I'll call my agent tomorrow and grovel for more work. Maybe I could get a part-time job in the Market, too."

"But that means you're making yourself unavailable for acting gigs. No, I won't hear of it. I'll take on more Uber shifts."

"Have I told you lately that you're the best?" Mum asked.

"You have. But you can never say it too much." They put their foreheads together and stayed like that until Templeton barked a greeting from the doorway.

"Hey, Wil. I was just putting on the kettle for tea," said Mum with a big smile. She really is a very good actress.

"What's up?" said Mup. "You look like you've got something on your mind."

"I do," I replied. "I just wanted to say . . ."

They waited.

"That I'm lucky to have you as my parents. And that I love you both very much."

The hugs and kisses went on for far too long.

"Why didn't you tell us about the money before?" Alex said the next day after school. He and Fabrizio walked a few meters ahead of me because they were headed to Alex's house, but technically I was still supposed to be walking by myself. It was overcast and a bit warmer; our winter coats were unzipped, and we had to dodge piles of slush. Fab wore a pair of mirrored sunglasses.

"I don't know," I said. "It's embarrassing."

"Could you ask Sal?" asked Fabrizio.

"Definitely not. He has his house, but other than that I think he lives on his social security checks. He jokes that he can't afford to live past ninety."

"What about your job?" asked Alex.

"I've done the calculations," I hollered up to them as we neared Spadina Ave. "I work twice a week, Thursday nights and Saturdays. A total of fifteen hours. I get paid minimum wage, so, even if I use every penny, I'll still have a significant shortfall—"

Alex stopped in the middle of the sidewalk, next to a guy in a hot dog suit. The hot dog was trying to wave people into a fast food joint. "Wait . . . did you say you're paid minimum wage?" Alex asked.

I nodded. The hot dog nodded, too.

"But you got a promotion a few months ago, right?"

"Yeah."

"That didn't come with a raise?"

"No. But it *did* come with more responsibility, which my boss said was even better."

Fab looked at me over the rims of his mirrored sunglasses. "You actually fell for that?"

"Um . . ."

The hot dog put his head in his oversized hands.

Alex gave me a pained looked. "Wil. He fed you a crock of turds. You need a raise. Like, yesterday!"

The hot dog nodded.

"I see your point. But I don't think Mr. Chernov is going to offer me one anytime soon—"

"Of course he won't offer it!" said Fab. "You have to ask."

"Oh. Oh, no. I—no."

"When's your next shift?" asked Alex.

"Tomorrow at noon."

"Do you have your boss's number?"

"Yes, but—"

"Call him right now. Ask to meet him at eleven thirty. This is the perfect opportunity for you to put some of your newfound confidence to work!"

I pulled out my phone. Then I stopped. "Guys, I don't think I can—" Alex grabbed my phone. "No! Do not put my phone down your pants again, *please*—" I tried to grab it back, but he just ducked out of my way and stood behind a *Toronto Star* box. When I tried to follow, Fab *and* the hot dog guy stood in my way.

Alex scrolled through my contacts. "Mr. Chernov, right?" He pressed Call, then put it on speaker and held it out to me.

We heard Mr. Chernov's voice. "This is Oleg Chernov. I can't take your call right now—you know the drill." *Beep.*

I stared at the two of them, frozen. Alex rolled his eyes. "Hello, Mr. Chernov?" he started. "This is your highly valued employee, Wilbur Nuñez-Knopf. I'd like to meet with you tomorrow at the restaurant before my shift starts. Say, eleven thirty? I have an important matter to discuss. Please text me to confirm you got this. Thank you so much, see you then, byeeeeeeeeeee!"

Alex hung up.

"That—you—you just impersonated me."

They both just grinned. Alex handed me back my phone. They kept walking. I fell back into step a few meters behind.

The hot dog guy gave me an enthusiastic thumbs-up.

At aquacise the next morning I was a bucket of nerves. I couldn't "dance like no one is watching," which is another one of Mup's favorite expressions, because I was terrified my bowels might let loose and the pool would have to be evacuated.

I managed to get through class. Afterward, while I waited for Sal to do up the buttons on his shirt, I checked my phone.

I had a text message from Mr. Chernov, confirming our meeting.

I told Sal all about it when we walked over to the ROM.

"I'm going to tell you a story, Wilbur," he said as we made ourselves comfortable under Fulton. "When I was first sent to live with that family in England, I was terrified. Quiet and obedient. But after a time, I started asking for small things. Nothing outrageous. An extra blanket at night. A second serving of potatoes if I was still hungry. Sometimes they said yes, sometimes they said no. Sometimes they beat me."

"They *beat you*?"

"But that was the worst thing that would happen. I'd get a *no*."

"Or a *beating*—"

"My point is, I learned that my voice mattered. By the time I got to Canada, I'd developed a pretty good voice, and sometimes I didn't just ask. Sometimes I insisted." He turned his head to look at me. "If you don't stand up for yourself, no one else will. You are your own best advocate."

"You make it sound so simple."

"It isn't. But remember what we talked about. It's all about how you present yourself. You may feel like a quivering mess on the inside but ask your boss for a raise like you think you deserve it. Because you *do* deserve it. Confident people make others have confidence in them."

"Sal. Wilbur." José loomed over us.

"Hi, José." Sal held out his hands. José pulled him to his feet and handed him his fedora. "Oh, I have more goodies for you." Sal reached into his canvas tote and handed José a baggie.

José grinned. "Peanut brittle. My favorite."

"I eat that stuff, I'll break a crown." Sal indicated his teeth.

"Thanks, Sal."

The two of us made our way toward the exit. Sal put a hand on my shoulder. "Remember, Wilbur: you are terrific."

"Radiant."

Then, in unison: "Some pig."

". . . so, what I'm trying to get at, sir, is that, well, I think I've been doing a pretty decent job for you, and so I'm wondering— I mean, only if it's possible—"

"For the love of—spit it out, kid, I'm a busy man," said Mr. Chernov. He ran a hand over his comb-over and leaned back in his office chair. I sat across from him. Above us the fluorescent lights emitted their continual buzz. The walls were bare except for a few *Sports Illustrated* swimsuit issue centerfolds, which felt like all kinds of wrong.

I'd rehearsed my speech during my walk down to Queen Street. I'd sounded good. Confident. Maybe even radiant and terrific.

But in front of Mr. Chernov, it had fallen apart. Or rather, *I* had fallen apart. "You currently pay me the minimum hourly wage. I'd like to ask if it's possible for me to get a raise."

"What? Speak up."

"I'd like a raise."

His bushy eyebrows shot straight up. "A raise!" He slapped his forehead. "Kid walks in and asks for a raise!" I shrank in my seat. "You must have balls the size of a gorilla."

"No, sir, just—normal-sized balls, at least, as far as I know—"

"You think I'm made of money?"

"Well, no. We are all made of molecules, my old friend Stewart told me that—"

"Why do you want a raise?"

I could actually feel the sweat dripping from my pits. "Well, specifically, I'm saving for a school trip. But generally, I'm asking because I've been here for over a year. I work hard for you. I supervise the other employees—"

"You're not getting a raise."

I slouched farther down in my chair. I'd hardly had any courage to begin with, and now it was officially used up. "Okay. I'll see myself out—"

"But I like you," he continued. "You're a hard worker." He smoothed his pencil mustache with his pinkie finger, thinking. "Here's what I'm going to do. I'm going to give you more shifts. You can work Saturdays *and* Sundays, and a couple more evenings a week on top of your regular shifts. Hopefully that will help pay for this trip of yours. And I'll try to give you overtime, how's that sound?"

"Will I get paid extra for the overtime?"

"Hell no! You know what my profit margins are like?" Then he leaned in conspiratorially and lowered his voice. "But here's what else I'm going to do for you. I'm going to promote you."

"Um. You already promoted me, sir, I'm a Submarine Sandwich Creation *Expert*." I showed him the plastic badge on my uniform.

He paused. Blinked. For a moment I wondered if he'd forgotten he'd done that. But then he said, "Well, now I'm going to make you a Submarine Sandwich Creation . . . *PhD*." He slapped his hands down on his desk triumphantly. "You're the first, Wilbur. The very first. You may not think it's worth anything right now, but I promise you, when you put that on a résumé, it's gonna stand out. Congratulations."

"Wow. Thank you, sir."

As I left his office, Mr. Chernov shouted after me: "Balls the size of a gorilla!"

SWEAT

ALEX SAID LATER THAT night. "You're doing more work. For the same hourly pay."

"Yes."

"And you see this as a victory."

"A partial victory, yes. I did the math, and I should make just enough to pay for the rest of the trip before we leave."

"Then congratulations, I guess." He finished setting up his keyboard.

I was in Alex's rec room for the first time in ages. It's an awesome space with orange shag carpeting, orange beanbag chairs, and a huge collection of his and his parents' LPs. I was pretty sure I was only there because Fabrizio had had to fill in for a sick actor at his dad's dinner theater, but so what? As a beggar, I couldn't be a chooser. Alex's parents were at the opera, and he'd whipped us up a delicious shakshuka, which was a very fancy egg dish he'd seen Yotam Ottolenghi make on TV, for a late dinner.

"Anyway, you did it," said Alex. "You stood up for yourself." He held up his glass of iced tea.

"Well . . . I sort of *stooped* . . . but still." I held up my glass too, and we clinked them in a toast.

We ran through a couple of our songs, and even though I still hated the sound of my voice, it was fun.

"The band is back together," Alex said with a laugh.

"We're like Paul and John from the Beatles," I said. "And Fab is, like, our Yoko Ono."

Alex stopped laughing. "Why do you dislike him so much, Wil?"

I blinked. "Sorry, what? Who?" He just gave me a hard stare. "I don't dislike Fab."

"Please. Wilbur—I *know* you. You don't have a poker face. Your feelings are so obvious."

I struggled to explain. "I don't know. You and I—for a while there—I thought we were really good friends."

"We were. We *are*—"

"But then Fab came into the picture, and *poof!* It was like I didn't exist. You just cut me out of your life."

"That's not true—"

"It totally is! Think about it. When was the last time you had me over?"

". . . last month—?"

"November fifteenth. It's now March."

Alex absorbed that. "Okay. Your point is taken. I did go rather cuckoo for Cocoa Puffs when Fab and I first got together."

"Yeah, you did—"

"But I also tried to invite you to do things with us. And every time, you'd be kind of rude."

"That's not true—" I began. Then I remembered the time they'd invited me to watch *Rocketman* with them.

"I always thought Elton John wrote his own lyrics," Fab had said afterward.

I'd snorted. "Seriously? Everyone knows it was Bernie Taupin."

"Well, I didn't. But I didn't grow up with Elton's music. Not exactly my era."

"Your *era*? Anyone who knows anything about music knows Elton is *timeless*."

Then there was the time Alex and I had tried to teach him how to play Carcassonne. I'd lost it. "For the last time, your meeple can be a knight, or a farmer—he can't be a *fashionista,* dummy!"

I had a few more rapid flashbacks in succession. Like the time I first saw Fab in his red pleather pants: "I love how you wear whatever you want, without caring what other people think." Or the time I said to him, "Is your voice naturally that loud, or is it your theater training?"

"I guess . . . ," I said. "I guess I was kind of a jerk. I guess I felt like he was stealing you away."

We were both quiet for a moment.

"It doesn't have to be either-or, you know," Alex said. "I can have a boyfriend *and* a best friend."

"I already have a best friend," I said. I knew I sounded like a petulant baby.

"Well, maybe you can have *two* best friends. I'm willing to give it a try if you are."

"Deal."

We sealed it with our secret handshake.

"I've been wanting to show you something," I said. "I have a new poem. It's called 'Charlotte's Web.'" I handed him my notebook.

Alex read it. "It's good, Wil."

"You think so?"

"I do." For the next half hour he plunked out the start of a melody while I sang off-key.

When we were bored with that, we decided to watch an episode of *Parts Unknown*. I flopped down into one of the beanbag chairs. "Chips!" I shouted. "My kingdom for some chips!"

"Oh, no, my friend," said Alex. "No chips for you." He pointed to some old weights and a bench in the corner, stuff his dad had bought but that no one ever used, including us. "Tonight, we are going to do a workout while we watch, *then* eat chips."

I groaned. "Come on. It's been a long day. And I already had a good workout at aquacise—"

"Wilbur. No offense. But you are approximately sixty years younger than anyone else in that class. It is not a workout. It's 'range of motion' for the elderly, to reduce their chances of breaking a hip." He pulled me to my feet and handed me a set of weights.

"Whoa, these are heavy."

"They're five pounds each. C'mon, I'm going to do them, too. I got the routine from one of Fab's self-help books."

Alex and I did repeat rounds of bicep and tricep curls, something called *the butterfly,* abdominal crunches, and push-ups. After a half an hour of this insanity I asked, "Can we rest now? My muscles are on fire."

"Mine are, too!"

He ran upstairs and came back down with a bag of chips. We flopped down into the beanbag chairs and tore it open. "I'm glad that's over," I said as I stuffed a handful of pickle-flavored heaven down my throat.

"Oh, but it isn't," he grinned, his mouth full of chips. "It's only just begun."

The next morning at eight a.m., Templeton and I ran toward the lakeshore with Alex. Well, Templeton ran. Alex and I shuffled. The sky was flat and gray. I ran through a puddle and got a soaker in the first couple of minutes.

"This—is—horrible!" I squeezed out as I tried to gulp in some air. I'd dug out a pair of ancient sweatpants and wore a windbreaker over a moth-holed T-shirt; I unzipped the windbreaker, already sweating.

"The worst!" Alex gasped. He looked more presentable, in a navy blue Adidas track suit, paired with a neon yellow sweatband to keep his hair from flopping into his face. His watch beeped. "Phew—we get to walk for one minute."

"How long did we run for?"

"One minute."

"Ugh! It felt like forever."

"But that's how we build up. One minute run, one minute walk."

"I don't think I can—"

"That's the language you have to stop using, that *I* have to stop using. I read all about this in one of Fab's books. *Run Your Way to Happiness.* It says not only is running good for your health; it's good for your mental health—something about endorphins—and that we need to reframe how we think—oops, minute's up." We started running again. "Plus it's something we can do together."

"I guess." I thought of all the other things I'd rather we do together, like play board games, go to movies, play music, lounge in his beanbag chairs doing absolutely nothing—anything would beat this. Templeton was having a great time on his four stubby legs; I was almost puking on my two. "How long do we do this for?" I wheezed.

"Thirty minutes total."

By the time we hit ten minutes—which was just five minutes of running—I was dying. I had to stop to catch my breath. Templeton and Alex were forced to stop with me. I was doubled over, trying not to puke up my morning bagel, when someone said, "Wilbur?"

I looked up. It was Mitzi, her long, red hair pulled back into a ponytail. She was in full running gear, earbuds in. "Hi," I managed on an exhale.

"I didn't know you were a runner," she said.

"He's not," Alex said cheerfully. "Neither of us are. First time out!" He introduced himself.

"Well, good for you," she said. "It gets easier, kind of."

Templeton started barking for attention. "Hi, wiener." She bent down and scratched his ears. "What's his name?"

I opened my mouth to respond.

And barfed a little onto one of her bright blue shoes.

Alex's eyes opened wide.

Mitzi glanced from me to the barf. She rubbed her shoe in a patch of snow. "See you at work." And off she ran, looking like a gazelle.

Alex burst into peals of laughter. "You barfed on her shoe!" he said, like he thought I'd somehow missed it. Then his watch beeped, and he started running again. "C'mon, Wil, get your butt in gear! Twenty minutes left to go!"

Later, at work, I told Mitzi Templeton's name, and apologized for puking on her shoe. She just shrugged and said, "What's a little barf between friends?"

It was one of the nicest things anyone had ever said to me.

STYLE & GROOMING

TIME WENT BY IN A FLASH. JUST A FEW WEEKS EARLIER I had been in a heartbroken funk; now, even if I wanted to wallow, I couldn't fit it in.

Alex, Templeton, and I did a run/walk three mornings a week. After school I either worked at Foot Long or went over to Sal's. He was doing his best to teach me some basic French.

"Where is the bathroom?"

"Où sont les toilettes?"

"Excuse me, do you speak English?"

"Excusez-moi, parlez-vous anglais?"

"I am warm."

"Je suis chaud."

He shook his head. "For the hundredth time. It's *j'ai chaud*. I *have* warmth. You just said, 'I am horny.'"

He also loaned me translated novels by famous French

authors, like *The Stranger,* by Albert Camus, and *The Hunchback of Notre-Dame,* by Victor Hugo.

Charlie texted me often, and I kept my promise to check in with Alex and Fab first before responding. It didn't take me long to get the hang of it; I sent her a *lot* of bland emojis.

Alex also started inviting me over on the weekends more often, along with Fabrizio. I knew it was a kind of test: Could the three of us hang out without one of us (hint, usually me) acting like an ass? Mostly, we could, even if Fab was still hopeless at Carcassonne.

One night, after we'd played a frustrating game of Scrabble (Fab insisted that *farkly*—a combination of *fun* and *sparkly*—was a word), Alex said, "Come on, Wil, let's play a few songs for Fab."

"Nope. No way. I sing for no one."

"Just one song. 'Charlotte's Web.'"

"No."

"Please," said Fab. "No judgment, I promise."

"Seriously? You're always judging me."

"True, but that's because we're on a mission, Wilbur. If you sing for me, I promise I'll keep any judginess to myself."

"This is a perfect and safe way for you to work on your self-confidence," coaxed Alex.

Eventually I caved. We performed "Charlotte's Web" for an audience of one.

When we were done, Fabrizio had that familiar look on his

face, like he was sucking on a lemon. "You don't have a great voice."

"I know—"

"And you keep your eyes closed way too much."

"Okay, well—"

"And you sometimes get this look on your face like you're straining to poop—"

"Okay! I thought you said you'd keep your judginess to yourself—"

"But aside from all that? It wasn't terrible. It's a good song. The music, the lyrics . . . I'm impressed."

Coming from Fab, this was high praise indeed.

Five weeks into my regimen, the four of us met up at my house after aquacise. We had the place to ourselves; Mup was still teaching at the JCC, and Mum, who had gotten the gig as "Receptionist," had to go in for a wardrobe fitting.

Sal pulled out all the treats the ladies had given us and put them on our Formica table for us to enjoy. Then they sat me on a kitchen chair while Sal put newspaper on the floor. "I cut my dad's hair all the time," said Alex. "You're in safe hands with me."

"But your dad hardly has any hair," I began, just as I saw the first swath of dark, wiry curls hit the floor.

I tried not to panic as more and more tufts of hair landed at my feet. It freaked Templeton out too, because he barked at the tumbleweeds but didn't dare touch them.

When Alex was done, he handed me a mirror.

It was like I was staring at another person. I looked . . . not half-bad. My face was still my face. But still. "It looks amazing. It's like you made me less . . ."

"Asymmetrical?" asked Fab.

"Yes!"

Alex beamed.

Once we'd swept up my hair, we traipsed upstairs. I carried Templeton. Fabrizio took in my bedroom. "I love the decor," he said, gazing at my posters of poker-playing dogs and Hermione Granger.

"Really?"

"No." He sat on my bed while Sal and Alex perched in the window seat.

"You look fitter than you did a month ago, Wil," said Alex.

"Which means your clothes look even worse on you than they did before," Sal added. He saw my pained look. "Sorry, but when you're my age, you call it like you see it."

"We'll make a *keep* pile and a *toss* pile," said Fab.

He and Alex headed into my closet. They tossed heaps of clothing onto my bed while Templeton barked. Sal started picking up items for inspection. He began with my all-time favorite gray sweatshirt. "Verdict?"

"Revolting," said Fab.

"Toss," said Alex, and Sal threw it onto the floor.

"Um, I wear that a lot—"

"And these," said Alex. He held up my beige pants and waggled his finger through a hole in the bum. "Why, Wilbur?"

"I figured I'd patch up the hole eventually—"

"On a pair of hideous, ancient, shapeless pants?" Alex tossed them onto the floor.

"You know that expression *clothes make the man*?" asked Sal as he picked through the heap of discards. "What do you think these clothes say about you?"

"That I have more important things to think about than fashion—" I started.

"That you have no respect for yourself. That you're trying to disappear," said Sal.

"That you've given up on life!" Fabrizio added, as he and Alex threw item after item onto the floor.

"Hey, no way am I tossing that." I plucked an oversized light brown sweater from the floor. Fab grabbed it from my hands. I saw him signal to Sal.

Sal opened the window. Fab threw the sweater. Sal caught it—

And tossed it right out the window.

"I—you can't—"

"Aaaaagh, these are disgusting!" Fabrizio had opened my top drawer. He held up a pair of my ancient, droopy underwear. "These are the color of hopelessness. The shape of loneliness."

He pulled out the drawer, ran to the window—and emptied the entire contents onto our front yard.

When we were done, I looked at my bed. Aside from a couple of T-shirts, the rest of my clothes were all discards. "Great. Now I literally have nothing to wear in Paris. I'll be walking around the city pants-less! I'll look like Winnie the Pooh!"

"Let's go to my place," said Sal.

"Why—"

"Just come."

The four of us—five, if you count Templeton—made our way next door. "You boys wait in the living room," he said to Alex and Fabrizio.

The two of us climbed the stairs to the second floor, going at Sal's pace, which was on par with a snail's. Photos of Irma lined the wall. There was a photo from their wedding day, a photo of them dancing, a photo of the two of them in Paris. I stopped and stared at that one. They were on a bridge, holding each other tight. "You two made such a handsome couple."

"We surely did."

He motioned me into his study, which was the mirror image of my bedroom. Cardboard boxes littered the floor. "What's all this?" I asked.

"I've been death cleaning."

My eyes widened. "What?"

"Book I read, by a Swedish woman. Talks about getting rid of a lot of your possessions *before* you die, so your loved ones don't have to do it all after you're gone."

"But you're nowhere near—"

"I'm eighty-five—"

"Years young! Sal, *please* stop talking about death."

"You do realize that death is one of the few certainties in life—"

I slapped my hands over my ears. "La-la-la-la-la-la-la!"

"That is excessively juvenile, Wilbur, but okay. I will move on." He opened the closet door. "Believe it or not, before I started to shrink, you and I were about the same height." Inside hung a row of suits. And not just any suits; even I could see that they were seriously classy.

"Wow . . . these are like the suits from that old TV show *Mad Men*."

"I wore one of these to my furniture shop every day. I was going to pack them away and send them to a thrift store, but then I thought, now that you've trimmed down somewhat, they might just fit you." He pulled a dark gray suit out and handed it to me. "Try it on. I'll wait downstairs."

I changed into the suit and walked downstairs.

Alex's eyes widened and he started to laugh. Fab clapped a hand over his mouth.

"Wowee," said Sal. "Wowee zowee."

I was genuinely confused. "Are these good reactions, or bad reactions?"

"Good!" Alex clarified.

"When Sal said you were trying on one of his suits, I thought, *Oh, no, an old-man suit*," said Fab. "No offense, Sal."

"None taken."

"But this is seriously retro cool."

"Very," Alex agreed.

"We have just one thing left to do," said Fab. "Just like they do on *Queer Eye*, we need to set up"—he did jazz hands to emphasize—"the reveal."

THE REVEAL

THE NEXT MORNING, ALEX, TEMPLETON, AND I WENT OUT for our run/walk. We could now go five whole kilometers alternating between four minutes of running at a glacial pace and one minute of walking. Spring was well and truly in the air; I even saw some buds on the trees.

When I got home, the house was quiet; the Mumps were having one of their long Sunday lie-ins which, now that I was older, I understood was code for "sex."

The guys weren't due to come over for another hour. I went upstairs and had a quick shower. I stood naked in front of the mirror and looked at my physique. I did look different. I swore that, when I held up my arm and tensed it, I could see an actual muscle trying to push its way out.

I did the dash to my room in my birthday suit. I put on a pair of my new Kelvin Cline underwear—a three-pack had cost only $9.99 at my local dollar store. Then I opened my closet. I had taken three of Sal's suits, plus some dress shirts and socks.

"These are so perfect," Fab had said. "You can dress them up or down. Wear the pants with a T-shirt or a sweater. Or slap on a dress shirt and a jacket and tie and go full class act."

I hadn't had the heart to remind them that I no longer had any casual pants, or sweaters, and only two T-shirts, because they'd tossed them all.

I was still deciding which suit to put on when the doorbell rang.

I threw on my ratty bathrobe, took the stairs two at a time, and opened the door. Fab stood on the doorstep, alone. "You're early," I said.

"Hello to you, too."

We stood staring at each other. "Um, are you going to invite me in?"

"Oh. Sure." Fab stepped inside. He held up a shopping bag. "Sal's suits are amazing. But you need a bit of casual stuff, too. So, I went to my local thrift store. . . ." He pulled a pair of jeans and three T-shirts out of the bag. "You can try them on for size. Oh, and I also got you this, because every person needs one signature piece." He pulled out a beautiful, lightweight, dark green sweater. "Trust me, this color is *you*."

I stood with the pile of clothes in my hands. "I don't know what to say."

"How about, thanks?"

"Of course. Thank you. But why?"

"I've invested a lot of time and energy in this experiment, Wilbur. My reputation is at stake. I can't have you walking around Paris looking like a great big Fashion Don't."

"But—how much did all this cost?"

"Almost nothing. It was fill-a-bag-for-twenty-bucks day."

"I'll pay you back—"

"Sure, whenever."

My eyes stung a little. "May I hug you?"

"You may."

We hugged. "Alex is lucky to have you as his boyfriend."

"I know," he replied. "He really is."

Alex and Sal arrived a while later. They herded the Mumps into the kitchen for my grand entrance.

I walked down the stairs, dressed in the dark gray suit. Fab had given me a jar of one of his old hair products; I'd used that, too.

They had perfect reactions. They looked surprised—then impressed—then moved. "Wil," said Mum. "You look so handsome!"

"So mature!" added Mup. We hugged. They both cried a little.

From his perch at the kitchen table, Sal beamed.

Fab recorded it all on his phone. "We *so* deserve our own TV show!"

I looked at myself in the hall mirror. I saw someone who stood up straight. Who wore clothes that didn't hide his body. It wasn't a perfect body. It wasn't a perfect face.

But it was me. And for the first time in ages?

I liked what I saw.

THE *MERDE* HITS
THE FAN

The match is on
The game is set
Then a curveball is thrown
Smacks me right in the head

from "Out of the Blue" by Wilbur Nuñez-Knopf

THE NEXT WEEK FLEW PAST. I WORKED MY EXTRA SHIFTS at Foot Long, and I gave Mr. P more installments toward the trip. I only had five hundred dollars to go. I went to band practice, I ran or lifted weights with Alex, and I took French lessons with Sal.

On Saturday morning, with just two weeks left before my departure, Sal and I stood in the change room after aquacise. We'd both just stripped down to nothing.

"Getting excited about Paris?" he asked me.

"I haven't had time to get excited." I got his clothes out of his locker and put them in a neat pile on the bench beside him.

"Aw, shoot," he said. "I'm sorry, Wilbur, but I have to whizz."

"No worries." I took his arm and walked him to the urinals, both of us buck naked. He held on to my arm with one hand and aimed with the other while I looked away. It was nothing I hadn't done for him before.

"Wank."

My insides curdled. It was bad enough having to hear that voice, and that word, Monday to Friday at school. But my weekends had always been sacred.

Of all the change rooms in all the cities in all the world . . .

Tyler Kertz had to walk into mine.

He stood a few meters away, in a Speedo like mine, although the similarities ended there. All of my efforts in the past weeks suddenly felt laughable. Tyler had actual six-pack abs. He looked like a shorter Michael Phelps.

It was like I'd sprung a leak. All my confidence and good feels oozed out. "Why are you here?" My tone was accusing.

"Swim practice. Our regular pool is closed for service today." His gaze drifted to Jeremiah, who was still in shrinkage mode from the pool.

He smirked.

Sal had finished at the urinals and turned around.

Tyler's smirk got even smirkier.

I wanted to kick him in the nuggets. Instead, I walked Sal to the sinks so he could wash his hands.

"This your grandpa?"

"No. This is my best friend. Sal Goldstein. Sal, this is Tyler Kertz."

Sal didn't say a word. He grabbed a paper towel and carefully dried his hands.

Tyler is a master at behaving like a normal, decent human being around adults. "Pleased to meet you, sir."

Fully naked, Sal turned and fixed Tyler with a steely gaze. "The feeling isn't mutual."

"I'm sorry?"

"I've heard about you. Taking pleasure in making my friend's life miserable." He turned to me. "You've got nothing to worry about, Wilbur. I've known guys like this all my life. He's a putz."

For perhaps the first time in his life, Tyler Kertz was speechless.

Sal put his hand on my arm. We slow-walked back to our lockers with as much dignity as we could muster, which, given that we were totally naked, was not a lot.

Miraculously, I felt okay again.

Not great; but okay.

Sal had patched up the leak before all the air could seep out.

"You are truly the best friend a guy could have," I said to him later as we lay under Fulton.

"Thank you, Wilbur. You're a great friend as well." We were quiet for a while, lost in our own thoughts. "I wanted to say something to you."

"Okay."

"You're still at the beginning of your life—"

"Not really, Sal, I'm fourteen—"

"At my age, that's still the beginning. Now please shut up. I'm trying to impart some old-man wisdom."

I shut up.

"Whatever happens on your trip—whatever happens with Charlie—just remember, you're going to *Paris*. This journey is about so much more than a girl. It's about expanding your horizons, your mind, your heart . . . you will remember this trip for the rest of your life. It is a tremendous thing."

"Not as tremendous as Fulton."

"Don't be a smart-ass."

"Sorry."

A shadow loomed over us. "Sal. Wilbur."

"José," said Sal. He held out his hands. José hoisted him to his feet and handed him his fedora. I got up on my own. Sal reached into his tote bag. "Another one of your favorites today. Oat fudge bars." Sal handed José a few bars from his stash.

José took the bars. "My wife complains I'm putting on weight."

"Just tell her there's more of you to love," said Sal.

José grinned. "I'll do that. Have a great day, Sal."

"You too, José."

I arrived at Foot Long just in time to start my shift at noon. Mitzi and Dmitry were scheduled to start then, too. Mitzi arrived on time.

Dmitry arrived at twelve-thirty.

"You're late," I said when he waltzed in.

He didn't even answer. He just yawned and yanked up his jeans so that they revealed only a third of his butt.

Mitzi rolled her eyes.

"Go and check the bathroom and make sure it's clean."

"Figured you'd have done that by now, Willoughby."

"Wilbur. And you figured wrong."

"I've told you about my psoriafungalitis."

"Which is a lie. You never brought me a note from your doctor."

"I have it."

"Where is it?"

"In the back."

"Then go and get it."

Dmitry returned a few minutes later, in uniform, and handed me a note. "This is written on a Foot Long napkin," I said. "You must think I'm a complete idiot."

He grinned. "You said it, Willard. Not me."

"Go and clean the bathroom," I said again, trying my best to sound forceful.

"Hmm, let me think, nah," said Dmitry. He stuck a finger into his ear and wiggled it around.

I glanced at Mitzi, who was watching both of us closely. I took a deep breath. I willed myself to speak with confidence. "I'm technically your boss. And I'm asking—no, *telling*—you to do it." Dmitry stared at me. I stared back. My heart was pounding in my chest. I was determined not to blink, but it was really hard. My eyes started to water. A Muzak version of Drake's "Know Yourself" was playing.

To my surprise, Dmitry blinked first. "Fine." He disappeared down the hall.

"Way to go!" Mitzi thumped me on the shoulder so hard I lost my balance and almost knocked over a vat of special sauce. "Sorry. It's all this CrossFit training I've been doing for the Pennsic Wars this summer. I don't know my own strength."

"No worries." I rubbed my shoulder. We slipped on our gloves and the two of us started prepping for the lunch rush in between customers, filling the bins with jalapeño peppers, banana peppers, olives, lettuce, tomatoes, cucumbers, and cheese. "How's Franklin?"

"He's great. Full of vim and vigor. Hey, I never told you I like your haircut."

I touched my head, pleased that she'd noticed. "Thanks."

"What's that song?"

I cocked my head to listen to the Muzak. The Drake song had ended. "I'm not sure."

"Not that one. The one you're humming."

I hadn't realized it, but I'd been playing "Charlotte's Web" in my head. "Just something I wrote."

"You write songs?"

"Well, no. I write poetry. My friend Alex is an amazing composer. He puts some of my poems to music."

"Cool."

A few minutes later she said, "Dmitry is taking a long time."

"Maybe he's just being thorough."

"Yeah. Maybe."

Dmitry finally reappeared, whistling tunelessly. He had a smug look on his face.

"Slice some buns," I told him. "I'm going to check out the job you did."

"Oh, I did a job all right," he said.

I headed to the back and opened the door to the unisex washroom.

The smell hit me first.

I put a hand over my nose and mouth and entered with trepidation.

I ventured a peek into the toilet bowl.

I gagged.

Mitzi was in the midst of Submarine Sandwich Creation for a customer when I returned. Dmitry was texting on his phone. "Go and flush that down immediately," I whispered.

"Pretty impressive, huh?"

"Now!" I hissed.

"I should take a photo. Send it to Guinness World Records."

A customer got up from his table, threw out his trash—and headed toward the bathroom.

I glared at Dmitry. "Move!"

He did not.

I had to get to the bathroom first. I moved to step around Dmitry, but he blocked my path. I tried again; he moved with me. Finally, I shoved him out of the way and ran down the hall—

I was too late.

A moment later the customer stepped out, his face a rictus of horror. "This place is disgusting." He pushed past me to the front doors. "I'm posting about it on Yelp!"

Dmitry thought it was hilarious. He was in a good mood all afternoon and into the evening, while I quietly fumed.

At eight-thirty, he went to the back and emerged a few minutes later in his street clothes.

"Where do you think you're going?"

"To a party." He slowed his voice down. "Par-tee. It's this thing where a bunch of people get together and talk and drink and have a good time—"

"Your shift doesn't end for another half hour."

"Twenty-eight minutes to be exact. It's dead quiet. You don't need me."

"That's not the point. You're getting paid for the time. So you're staying. Also, you were half an hour late." My insides were a quivering mess, but I kept my voice calm, like Sal had tried to teach me. "Start sanitizing the veggie bins."

Mitzi's eyes darted from me to Dmitry.

"You can't tell me what to do."

"Yes, I can. I am a Submarine Sandwich Creation *PhD*. You are a Submarine Sandwich Creation *Engineer*. I am your boss. And you will do as I say, or else."

Dmitry smirked. "Or else what?"

All of the work I'd done over the past number of weeks just crystallized. I couldn't believe the words that were coming out of my mouth. "Or else I'll fire you."

He burst out laughing. "You can't fire me."

"Yes, I can."

"No, you can't."

"Yes, I can—"

He opened the front door—

"You're fired!" I blurted. "Give me your badge." I held out my hand. It was shaking.

Dmitry stopped. "You've got to be joking—"

"Give. Me. Your. Badge!"

He stared at me, hard. Then he took his badge out of his jacket pocket and threw it. It skittered across the floor. "This isn't over."

He left.

I picked up his badge. I was jangly with nerves.

But I also felt exhilarated.

I had stood up to Dmitry. But more important, I had stood up for myself.

Mitzi stared at me. "You do realize you had no authority to fire him."

"I believe that is technically true."

She broke into a grin. "But who cares. 'Cos that was awesome." She put up her hand for a high five.

"I'd better let Mr. Chernov know. He'll need to hire someone new."

"He could hire a mop and it would be a step up from Dmitry," she said.

Which was both funny *and* true.

I arrived at work early the next morning, since I was scheduled for a double shift. The weather had turned nasty again, snowing a lot in the night, one last reminder of winter, even though technically it was spring. I didn't have a chance to shovel our walk or Sal's before I left.

I changed into my uniform. When I came out to the front, Mr. Chernov was sitting at one of the tables. "Mr. Chernov, hello. You must have gotten my text."

"I did. You fired Dmitry."

"Yes." The doors opened and Mitzi stepped inside, bringing a gust of cold air with her.

"Oh, hi, Mr. Chernov—" she began.

He held up a hand to stop her, his gaze fixed on me. "Why, exactly, did you fire him?"

I felt a surge of confidence, and I ran with it. "There were a number of reasons. He was the laziest person I've ever met."

"Really."

"Really. He barely did any work while he was here. Plus, he didn't take instructions. He showed up late and left early. He was disrespectful to me and the other employees."

"Go on."

"Honestly, sir, he was a total jerk."

"A jerk, huh." He drummed his fingers on the table.

"I know you value hard work—"

"And family."

"Of course. His family must let him get away with murder. They clearly haven't raised him with core values and ethics. He's one of the most entitled people I've ever met."

"Really."

I nodded.

Mr. Chernov had a vein in his forehead that throbbed when he got angry. It was pulsating right now, big-time. "What is my last name?"

"Chernov."

"What is Dmitry's last name?"

I thought for a moment; his badge just said *Dmitry*. "I'm not sure I've ever asked—"

"Chernov, you moron! His last name is Chernov! I'm his dad!"

Oh, crap.

"That *total jerk* is my son. So, since I'm the only one who can *actually* fire people, who do you think I'm going to keep, and who do you think I'm going to let go, *effective immediately*?"

I glanced at Mitzi, who stood frozen in the doorway. "Well, I'd like to think that you're motivated more by good business sense than by nepotism, so I'm going to say your son?"

"BAH!!!" he said, imitating a game show buzzer. "Wrong answer. You're fired. Give me your badge and get the hell out of my store."

I felt numb. "But, sir—I'm a Submarine Sandwich Creation *PhD*—"

"A made-up title that means diddly-squat! What kind of idiot takes on more work for not one cent more on his hourly wage?"

My ears were ringing. Mr. Chernov stood with his hand out, tapping his foot impatiently. My fingers fumbled at the clasp on my badge. I couldn't get them to work properly.

Mitzi approached. She took the badge off for me. She placed it into my hand, giving it a squeeze. "I wish I could quit in solidarity, Wilbur," she whispered. "But I need the money."

I handed my badge to Mr. Chernov. "Can I have my pay for the past two weeks—"

"Nope. No can do. The money you're owed will just about cover your uniform."

"But—I don't want the uniform. Why would I want the uniform?"

"You clearly didn't read the fine print in your contract. Uniform belongs to you."

"But I'm owed a few hundred dollars—"

"Uniform's worth about that much."

"Mr. Chernov. There is no way—"

"So hire a lawyer and sue me! Now get the hell out of here! GO!"

My stores of confidence were used up. I was too shocked to keep fighting.

I went to the back and grabbed my stuff. Then I walked out of Foot Long for the very last time.

The Charlie Brown Christmas theme music was playing through the speakers, like it had been cued up just for me.

When I got home, Templeton greeted me by dragging his butt across the floor. I groaned. "Oh, Templeton. I love you. But why right now? *Why?*"

Mum was at her laptop in the kitchen. She wore a pink wig and tons of makeup and a barely-there neon orange top with a black leather miniskirt; she was just home from an overnight on a low-budget horror flick. "How'd the shoot go?" I asked.

"Fine, I guess. I mean, as fine as it can be, playing Hooker #4 in yet another piece of misogynist crap."

I couldn't resist. "Did you feel like you prostituted yourself?"

"Ha-ha. Hilarious." She pulled off the wig and looked up from her laptop. "Ah, well. They went long, so at least I'll be paid overtime—" She stopped, giving me a puzzled look. "Why are you home? And in your uniform? I thought you were working until six today?"

I took a deep breath. "I got fired." I told her the entire story. My eyes got a little watery, to tell the truth. She stood up and put her arms around me.

"Oh, Wil. Your boss sounds like a jerk."

"I was good at my job, Mum. I really was."

"I don't doubt it for a second."

Then the worst part of all of this hit me. "Mr. Chernov owes me a lot of money. He says he isn't going to pay it."

"What?"

"I still owe Mr. P five hundred dollars, and we're supposed to go to Paris in less than two weeks."

"He *will* pay you. We'll make sure of that. But it might not be before you leave." She thought for a moment. "We'll figure this out, pickle. Mup's out driving Uber, but when she gets back . . . Just—let me get some sleep in the meantime, clear my head." She looked so tired.

She headed upstairs for a nap. I didn't feel like being alone, so I knocked three times on the wall.

Sal didn't knock back. This didn't surprise me; as far as he knew, I was still at work.

I texted him.

Can I come over?

No response.

Je peux venir chez vous?

Still no response. I figured he was probably out and about, enjoying his Sunday.

Then I remembered all the fresh snow, and the fact that I still hadn't shoveled his walk.

I went to the front door and looked outside. There were no footprints to or from his front door.

I got a bad feeling.

I tucked Templeton under my arm, grabbed Sal's spare key, and went next door. I knocked.

There was no answer.

He'd had pinochle the night before; I'd seen a cab drop him back at home at around ten p.m.

He had to be in the house.

I knocked again and rang the bell. "Sal?"

I let myself in. "Sal?"

No answer. I walked toward the kitchen. "If this is another intervention—"

Sal was lying on the linoleum floor.

I put Templeton down. We both rushed to him. I dropped to my knees and put a finger on his neck to check for a pulse.

There wasn't one.

The next ten minutes were the longest of my life.

I opened Sal's mouth and felt around to check if his airway was clear.

Then I fumbled for my phone and hit Emergency Call.

I started to perform CPR, or what I remembered of CPR from a babysitting course I'd taken when I was eleven.

"This is 911, do you need police, fire, or ambulance—"

"Ambulance. My friend—I think he's had a heart attack. He's not breathing."

"All right, sir, what's the address?"

I told her. "I'm doing CPR but I'm not sure I'm doing it right."

"Stay on the line, okay. I'll walk you through it. Ambulance is on its way."

She was really calm and really clear. I followed her instructions. I tilted his head back and covered his mouth with mine. Two breaths followed by thirty compressions. Two breaths, thirty compressions. I don't know how many times I repeated this. It felt like hundreds.

It also felt like ages before the paramedics came through the front door, but I was told later it was only six minutes.

They used a defibrillator on Sal. I stood back, hearing the *thwack* as it sent electrical currents to his heart. Templeton whimpered, and peed a little. I wanted to whimper and pee a little, too. I picked him up. It all felt like a terrible dream. Then Mum was beside me. The three of us held on to each other as the paramedics lifted Sal onto a stretcher and wheeled him to the ambulance. "Can I come with you?" I asked.

"Sorry, not enough room. We're taking him to Toronto General. You can follow us there."

Then the back doors closed, and the ambulance drove away.

"They didn't put on the siren," I said.

Which seemed like a really bad sign.

Sunk into a pit of darkness
Feeling dazed and comatose
Working at attempting normal
Impossible to even get close

From "Living Nightmare"
by Wilbur Nuñez-Knopf

MUM AND I STOOD ON THE SIDEWALK, BOTH OF US BARE-
foot. We stood there until we could no longer feel our feet. Then
Mum said, "I'll call Mup. She'll drive us to the hospital."

Mup picked us up ten minutes later. "I'm sure he'll be fine."
I noticed she was driving a little faster than she should. "I'm
sure he'll be fine," she said again, as if repeating it enough times
would make it true.

We waited at the hospital for a long time.

Eventually, a doctor came out to see us. "You're Sal Goldstein's
family?"

"Yes," I said, which didn't feel like a lie.

"No," said Mup. "But we're like family."

"Does he have any family members we should contact?"

Mum shook her head. "Not that we know of. His wife pre-
deceased him. We're his next-door neighbors."

"Are you the ones who found him?"

"Our son did."

The doctor turned her gaze on me. "Your timing was impeccable, young man. If you'd been five minutes later . . ." She let us figure out the rest of that sentence ourselves. "You saved his life."

"Is he going to be okay?"

"He's not out of the woods yet. He's in the ICU."

"Can we see him?" asked Mum.

"He's heavily sedated. I suggest you come back tomorrow."

I didn't want to leave, but the Mumps convinced me that it would be better for all of us if we got some rest. On the way home, I texted Alex to tell him what had happened.

By the time we pulled up outside our house, Alex was waiting for us. "Wil. I'm so sorry. I can't believe it," he said. We hugged. We cried. The Mumps ordered pizza from our favorite pizza joint, but nobody ate much.

Early the next morning, Alex stopped by to take Templeton out for a walk. The Mumps gave him a note to give to the office, explaining why I'd be missing school; then the three of us headed back to the hospital.

Sal was still in the ICU.

He looked like a tiny little bird. Tubes ran out of his nose and his arms. His eyes stayed closed. I don't think he had any idea that we were there. I squeezed his hand. "I love you, Sal. Please get well." Then I started blubbering again and the nurse suggested it was time for us to go.

When I got home, I broke one of Alex and Fab's rules and called Charlie. "Wilbur, this is so sad. It is like a bad dream," she said through tears. "I am so sorry. I wish I was there. For Sal but also for you."

We talked for a long time. She asked me to keep her posted, and I promised I would.

Fab and Alex came over later. "He's going to get better," said Fab, and even though none of us knew if that was true or not, we tried hard to believe it. "And when he gets better, there is no reason why he shouldn't look his best."

We let ourselves into Sal's house with my spare key. The three of us filled a leather bag with things we thought he might like to have. "We *must* bring one of his old-timey sweaters," said Fab. "The one with the elbow patches."

"And his fuzzy pink slippers, he loves those slippers," said Alex.

"And his gray fedora, just in case," I said. I also picked one of his favorite books, *The Amazing Adventures of Kavalier and Clay* by Michael Chabon, and added my own favorite, my worn copy of *Charlotte's Web*. We added the photo of him and Irma in Paris, clean underwear, a toothbrush, and his shaving kit.

All three of us went to the hospital the next day. We were greeted with good news: Sal had been moved to a regular ward. He was in a semiprivate room with a man who moaned a lot.

Sal already had company; Ruth Gimbel sat in the chair beside his bed, knitting. I'd only ever seen her in her swimsuit and bathing cap; her hair towered above her head in a sculpted beehive. She wore a floral print dress with big white orthopedic running shoes. "Wilbur, hello," she whispered. Sal was sleeping. He still looked really frail, but there was a little more color in his face.

"Hi, Ruth." I introduced her to Fabrizio and Alex.

At the sound of our voices, Sal's eyes fluttered open. He broke into a smile. "Hey. It's the Three Musketeers."

We showed him the bag we'd brought. He seemed particularly happy to see the photo of Irma, and we placed it on his bedside table. After a few minutes a nurse came in and told us there were too many of us in the room. "Maximum two visitors at a time," he admonished.

"I need to go to school this afternoon anyway," said Alex. "I have a math test." Alex and Fab said their goodbyes. Ruth stayed planted in the one and only chair.

Sal turned to me. "I hear you saved my life."

"I just did what anyone would do."

"That is patently untrue. Most people would freeze, or panic. You didn't. For a kid who thinks he doesn't have a lot of courage, this puts that lie to rest."

I took his hand. "I'm so glad you're here."

"Me too!" He managed a weak laugh, and then he started to cough.

Ruth leapt up and tried to get him to have some water from a sippy cup. "Now, Sal, don't overexert yourself—"

"Ruth, why don't you go get yourself something to eat in the cafeteria," Sal said.

"I'm good, I brought some knishes—"

"Ruth. Give Wilbur and me a bit of time alone, please."

Reluctantly, Ruth left, her big white orthopedic shoes squeaking with every step.

"That woman," said Sal. "Her heart is in the right place but she's making me crazy. The twins came by, too. Leah and Alice. Brought me enough cinnamon buns to feed a small army."

"You're a hot commodity."

He started to laugh.

And I started to cry.

Sal put his gnarled hand on top of mine. "Why the waterworks? I'm here thanks to you."

"You could have died. In fact I think you *were* dead when I came into the house—"

"Well then, this is the best possible outcome, isn't it?"

"Of course. It's just—" I couldn't finish my thought.

"It's just that it made you realize I *will* die."

I nodded, still sniffling.

"Wilbur. I have had a rich, long, full life. I'm not afraid of my death. And if I'm not afraid of it, you shouldn't be, either."

"But I'll miss you *so much.*"

"Good. It will be nice to be missed by someone when the time comes." He managed another weak smile. I could tell he was getting tired.

"I should let you rest."

"I suppose so." He smiled again. "Have you started packing for your trip yet? You leave in a week and a half, right?"

"Well, no."

There was a pause. "What do you mean?"

"I'm not going. Not now."

Sal closed his eyes, and for a moment I thought he'd fallen back to sleep. When he opened them again, he looked angry. "No. No, no, no. No way do you get to use me as your excuse not to go. I won't hear of it. Of course you're going."

"But—"

He gripped my hand with an alarming amount of strength, given the circumstances. "These past couple of months with you and your friends have been some of the finest of my life, Wilbur. Certainly the finest since Irma passed away. I refuse to see all of our hard work go to waste. So if you don't want to do it for you, do it for me. And write me a real letter. It's a dying art." He let go of my hand. "It will give me something to look forward to."

What could I say? I wasn't about to tell him that I'd lost my job and I didn't have enough money for the trip. I just nodded and headed for the door. Sal's voice made me turn back.

"We're born, we live a little while, we die."

It took me a moment.

He'd quoted Charlotte from *Charlotte's Web,* just before she died.

Which made me start crying all over again.

* * *

I went to school for the rest of the day in a fog. Tyler shouted something at me in the corridor, but it barely registered.

When I got home, Mum was in the kitchen in an old pair of overalls, staining an old chair she'd found in the back alley to sell on Etsy. She'd visited Sal that afternoon. "I think that woman Ruth has moved in!"

"She's had a mad crush on Sal since forever." I put on the kettle for tea. "Is there something different in here?" The kitchen felt emptier, but I couldn't put my finger on it.

She didn't answer. "Want some tea and cinnamon toast?" Cinnamon toast is the one thing Mum does really well; she doesn't skimp on the butter, or the sugar.

"Yes, please."

When we were done with our snack, I took Templeton out for a walk to the park. Lloyd and Viktor were on their favorite bench. "Hey, I heard about Sal," said Lloyd. "Heard you saved his life."

"How did you—"

"Word travels fast around the Market," said Viktor. "I like that guy. We always shoot the breeze when he comes in to get his cheese."

"He brings me his old *New Yorker* magazines," said Lloyd. "We discuss the articles."

I hadn't known Sal did that. Come to think of it, I had no idea how Sal spent his days while I was at school, which made me feel like a crap friend.

"How's he doing?" asked Viktor.

"Pretty good, I think. I saw him this morning."

Lloyd leaned forward. "Will you give him our best?"

"Of course."

"You're a hero, man," said Lloyd.

"No. I'm really not."

When I got home, Mup was in the kitchen, too; Mum was still working on her chair, and Mup was starting dinner. "Wil, come sit," said Mum. She took an envelope out of the bib pocket of her overalls and sat down with me at the table.

"What's this?"

"Open it and find out."

It was a check.

For five hundred dollars.

"Whoa. We can't afford this—"

"We can. I sold a bunch of my cookie jars on Etsy," said Mum. "It's amazing what collectors will pay."

I looked up. *That's* what was different. Her entire collection was gone. The owl, the mushroom, the smiley face, the Santa Claus, the sneaker, the carousel, all of them—gone. "But you love those cookie jars."

"Between you and the cookie jars? Not much of a contest."

Then all three of us got weepy again, because we felt sad and relieved and happy all at once. Mum broke into a rousing rendition of "Family Is Family" by Kacey Musgraves, and Mup and I joined in.

The next day I gave Mr. P my final payment.

About a week later I left for the airport, to fly to the city of Paris, in the country of France, on the continent of Europe, on the planet called Earth.

PARIS, JE T'AIME

My bags are packed
And so is my heart
Don't know what lies ahead
But I'm ready to start

from "Anyone's Guess" by Wilbur Nuñez-Knopf

THE MUMPS DROVE ME TO THE AIRPORT. I WORE A PAIR of Sal's pants and one of his suit jackets over the dark green sweater Fab had chosen for me. He was right—it really was my color. The jacket still smelled a bit like Sal; a combination of old books and spices. It made me feel warm and safe.

He was still in the hospital, but he seemed a little bit stronger every day, and the doctors said he should be able to go home soon. "Remember what I said to you before," he said to me during our last visit, "Whatever happens with Charlie: Have fun. Take in the beauty of the city. Stuff yourself full of croissants and pastries. Be open to new experiences." I vowed to take my best friend's words to heart.

Templeton sat on my lap in the back seat. "If you need to express his anal sacs," I said, "use a lot of Vaseline. And squeeze gently. *Gently—*"

"We've got it covered, pickle," said Mup.

"Passport?" Mum asked as we pulled up outside International Departures.

"Check."

"Instruments?"

"Check."

"Credit card in case of emergencies, travel insurance card, a raincoat, money belt, first aid kit, Gravol for motion sickness, TUMS for the rich French food, melatonin to help you with jet lag, Handi Wipes, clean underpants—"

"Norah," said Mup.

"It's all good, Mum."

We got my stuff out of the trunk. The two of them enveloped me in a hug. I towered over both of them. "You have a magnificent trip, dear sweet boy," said Mup. She was holding it together better than Mum.

Mum handed me a homemade cloth bag. "A care package for you. You can open it on the plane. And this is a little something for Charlie and her dad." She took a box out of her purse and opened it: inside were two small ceramic beavers, one with an *S* on its back, and one with *P*. "A very Canadian salt-and-pepper-shaker set."

"They'll love it." Both of them moved in for another hug. I finally had to wriggle free. "I have to meet the others inside." I kissed them both, told them I loved them, and walked into the airport, pulling my battered plaid suitcase with the wonky wheel behind me.

*　*　*

Once we'd all made it safely through security and to our gate, Mr. Papadopoulos stood on a chair to address us. He was a ball of nerves. "As the Trudeau-Manias, we represent our school. I expect you to be on your best behavior at all times. Especially around Geneviève—Mademoiselle Lefèvre." An airport employee came by and told him to get down off the seats. He did as he was told. "Does this shirt go with these pants?" he asked Fabrizio. He'd gone for a rather bold floral pattern that hugged his chest and torso.

"You're making a statement," said Fab, which was not exactly a compliment, but Mr. P beamed. I noticed he'd lost the goatee.

Tyler was nearby, talking to Olivia the oboist and periodically checking himself out in the window's reflection behind her like the narcissist he was. Seeing him still made my stomach twist into a pretzel. But with everything that had happened, the twisting didn't feel quite so intense.

I was half-excited, half-nervous when we boarded the massive Boeing 777. I'd only been on an airplane once, when we'd flown to Toronto from Vancouver, and I'd gotten motion sickness and had to use the barf bag. When I told Alex and Fabrizio this, they insisted I take the aisle seat. I sat down. My knees practically touched my face.

We lifted off. I watched an old movie called *Snakes on a*

Plane, which was probably not the best choice. But I didn't feel sick, not even a bit.

After they'd served our meal and the trays were collected, the lights were dimmed so people could sleep. Alex and Fab pulled a blanket over themselves, but they sure as heck didn't sleep. So I picked up my pack and moved farther back, claiming an empty row to myself.

I remembered the care package Mum had given me, and I pulled it out. Inside were some rock-hard spelt cookies, a small tube of hand sanitizer, a package of tissues—and an accordion strip of condoms. She'd stuck a Post-it Note on them: *Peanut, in my opinion you are still far too young to have sex, but it is always better to be prepared! And remember: ENTHUSIASTIC CON-SENT!* I appreciated the thought. At the bottom of the bag was a wrapped gift, with another note from Mum: *Found this last week at a garage sale. You'll look like a true Parisian!*

I opened it up; it was a slightly used red beret.

I went to the bathroom and tried it on. I set it at a jaunty angle. It *did* look rather good on me if I do say so myself.

When I got back to my seat, I slid the beret into my bag. I turned out my light, popped in some earplugs, pulled on my eye mask, and closed my eyes.

"I've been keeping an eye on you, Wank."

I pulled up my mask. Tyler stood over me. He spoke quietly, so only I would hear. "You've been working hard, haven't you?" I said nothing. "Ever heard the expression *You can't polish a turd*?"

"Yup," I said. "It's what the doctor said to your parents when you were born." *Zing!* I had no idea where that had come from; I usually only thought of good comebacks hours after I needed them.

"It's cute, in a way. All this work, hoping it might give you a shot with Charlie. But it won't help. She's seriously hot for me."

"Liar. She doesn't even like you."

He grinned. "Oh, Wank. I don't like her, either. She talks too much. She's not even that good-looking, to be honest. Her eyes are too small, and her hips are too wide. But I'm not after her *heart*." A wave of rage pulsed through my veins. I leapt to my feet. My head whacked the overhead bin.

"Ladies and gentlemen, the captain has put on the seatbelt sign as we're going through an area of turbulence," said a flight attendant on the overhead speakers. "Please return to your seats immediately and fasten your seatbelts. We're in for a bumpy night."

Tyler shot me one last smirk before heading back to his seat.

I fastened my seatbelt. Anger still coursed through my body, along with familiar bad thoughts about myself. I closed my eyes and repeated my mantra over and over again in an attempt to make the bad thoughts go away. "I love you. You are an incredible person. You are a winner!"

I kept repeating it until the man across the aisle implored me to shut up so he could sleep.

April 7

Dear Sal,

Well, I'm doing as you asked, and writing you a real,
honest-to-goodness letter. How are you, BFF? Do you
feel well? Is Ruth Gimbel still making you crazy? Do the
twins still visit you? Is Mum bringing you spelt cookies,
and do you try to hide them under your mattress?

    It's three o'clock in the morning over here and I'm
wide awake, but only because of the time change. So
instead of staring at the ceiling and waiting to fall back
to sleep, I decided I should tell you all about my first day
here in Paris.

    Charlie and the others met us at the airport, and

Sal, the moment I laid eyes on her, all my feelings just came flooding back. She gave me a massive hug. And of course she immediately asked about you. She loves you almost as much as I do!

We took a train into Paris, and Sal, get this: Charlie kept staring at me. Then she said, "You look different. Less like Napoleon Dynamite and more like . . . hmm, Justin Timberlake." If you don't know who JT is, look him up right now! It's high praise! Then she grabbed my arm and squeezed and said, "Wilbur, you have muscles!"

The French students live in different areas of the city, or arrondissements, *which I guess you already know about. Alex and Fab are staying in an area called Belleville. Charlie lives in an area called Le Marais. I had to lug my suitcase up the stairs at her Métro stop, because there are no escalators. We came out onto a busy Paris street. It was raining, and I was fuzzy with jet lag, so the truth is I didn't notice much of our surroundings as we walked to Charlie's apartment; everything just looked wet and gray.*

We walked down some narrow streets and then Charlie stopped outside an old wooden door that was painted bright blue. It had a big brass knob in the center that was shaped like a lion's head. She punched in a code and the door clicked open. We entered into a courtyard paved with cobblestones. Charlie said bonjour to an older woman who was watering some plants. Charlie told me that Madame Da Silva is the "Concierge," which is sort of like being a building superintendent—but again, I guess you know that already, since you and Irma were here so many times!

We headed through another door, and the two of us squeezed into a teensy and ancient elevator, which was suspended in a mesh cage in the middle of a winding staircase. It barely fit the two of us and my suitcase. The good news is, I didn't feel freaked out because we only had to go up a few floors. I was practically nose-to-nose with Charlie so I tried not to breathe out since I knew my breath must be seriously rank from the plane.

Charlie's apartment is on the fourth and top floor, and Sal, it is so cool. It has high ceilings and crown moldings and they even have a cherub painted on the ceiling! The living room has hardwood floors and built-in bookshelves covering one whole wall. You can throw open the windows to look down to the street below. Even though it's an old building, they have a modern (but tiny) kitchen and a modern (but tiny) bathroom. Weird thing: there are two toilets side by side in the bathroom. One looks normal and the other one looks like a toilet without a seat. It's a mystery.

I also met Minouche, Charlie's tortoiseshell cat. She's

very haughty and completely adorable—but don't tell Templeton I said so!

I have my own room, which used to belong to Charlie's au pair. It's tiny but perfect, with a narrow bed and a little desk and a chair. My window overlooks the courtyard.

After I unpacked and had a shower, Charlie gave me some lunch. At first I thought she'd cut the cheese— and she had, but literally, ha-ha! The cheese she served was super-stinky! I was afraid to eat it in case it tasted like farts too, but then I remembered that you told me to be open to new experiences, so I tasted it and WOW, I have never eaten such good cheese—or should I say, fromage—in my life!

After that I lay down for five minutes, but I must have fallen asleep, because next thing I knew Charlie shook me awake two hours later! It was time to meet up with the others. Mum gave me a red beret as a gift, so I put it on, but Charlie took one look at it and said, "NON." Actually, she pulled it off my head and flung it across the room, which felt a tad unnecessary. (Please don't tell Mum.)

It had stopped raining, and the sun was out. Charlie and I walked down the narrow streets, and it was like I was seeing everything with new eyes. We passed a small area of Jewish delis and Arab kebab shops, and

I thought of you, Sal, because, well, you're Jewish, but also because I am sure you and Irma have walked on the same streets. We passed shops selling clothing and fancy stationery and pens, and the most mouthwatering boulangeries and pâtisseries. It's like every shop has been art-designed! Charlie told me that Le Marais means "the marsh," and you can get a sense of what Paris must have looked like long ago, because in the 1800s, Napoleon III had most of the old city destroyed and replaced with wide boulevards and modern apartments. Le Marais was the only neighborhood he didn't touch, because only poor people lived there, and Napoleon III didn't care about them. But I guess you know this, too.

We crossed two bridges to get from the Right Bank to the Left Bank of the Seine. As far as my eyes could see I was looking at majestic old buildings. We stopped at a memorial that was erected for the Jewish children who'd been handed over to the Nazis by the Vichy government and murdered in concentration camps. Charlie told me that beauty and tragedy walk hand in hand in Paris.

We met the others for a boat tour on the Seine. Oh, Sal, it was incredible. We went past Hôtel de Ville, the Louvre, the Musée d'Orsay, the Grand Palais . . . then we rounded a small bend and there it was, the Eiffel Tower! I don't know how to describe the feeling of

*happiness that welled up inside me. I see why you and
Irma kept coming back here. I didn't even care when
Tyler sat on the other side of Charlie and tried to talk
to her; I was too busy staring at all the other beauty
around me.*

*When we got back to the apartment, Charlie's dad
was there. He is SO intimidating, Sal! He's short and
handsome with a lot of wavy dark hair and piercing
eyes. He was wearing a tweed jacket over a rumpled
shirt and jeans—he looked, well, like a famous French
intellectual! He made us omelets with asparagus and
goat cheese for supper. It was the best omelet I have ever
tasted.*

*Monsieur Bourget, or Guillaume, as he asked me
to call him (he keeps having to remind me it is not
pronounced "Gwillum" but "Geeyome," hard G), didn't
ask me any intellectual questions, PHEW. After dinner
he put on the TV and we watched an interview he'd
done for the late edition of the news. "I am talking
about the latest 'scandale' involving one of our French
politicians," he explained. I didn't understand a word,
but I watched to be polite. He put Minouche on his lap
and talked to her in a baby voice, which was funny
because his voice on TV is very deep and authoritative.*

*I fell asleep as soon as my head hit the pillow, but
I woke four hours later. Now it's four a.m. and I'm*

*starting to feel sleepy again, so I'll sign off now and try
to get back to sleep.*

*It's wonderful to be here, Sal. You are right—it is a
tremendous thing! I will keep you posted, on everything.
Thank you again for all your help and for convincing me
to go. I love you, Sal, and I think about you all the time,
hoping you are doing well.*

> *Your BFF,*
> *Wilbur*

*PS: I almost forgot, please tell the Mumps I gave
Guillaume their gift of the beaver salt-and-pepper set.
I told him the beaver was Canada's national animal.
He said,* "Ce sont les choses les plus laides que j'ai
jamais vues." *Which Charlie told me meant "This is the
loveliest gift I have ever received."*

Paris
Foreign, fascinating
Cafés, cigarettes, baguettes
Everywhere steeped in history
City of love

a cinquain by Wilbur Nuñez-Knopf

I WOKE FROM A DEEP SLEEP TO THE SOUND OF PURRING, and paws kneading my hair. When I opened my eyes, I was staring straight into Minouche's green ones. *"Bonjour!"* said Charlie from the doorway. "I sent in Minouche to wake you, because she does it so gently."

Sunlight streamed through the window. "What time is it?" I asked, groggy with sleep.

"Eight o'clock. We meet the others in one hour."

I had a shower, which made me feel a bit less dopey. Breakfast was fresh croissants, jam, yogurt, and coffee. Never in my life have I tasted such good croissants.

When we were done eating, Charlie went to her room to change. Guillaume turned to me and said in a stern tone, "Wilbur, come with me, please." He took me into the washroom and pointed at the second toilet. "You urinated in our bidet last night."

"Your what?"

He explained what a bidet is for.

"Seriously?" I asked.

"Seriously."

"Wow." Leave it to the French to invent a genital-and-bum washer!

"Do not piss in it again," he said.

I promised I would do no such thing.

Just before nine o'clock we left for the day. Charlie wore a hot pink minidress with white tights. I wore a pair of Sal's suit pants and one of his shirts. Charlie showed me how to wrap my dark green sweater casually yet jauntily around my neck. She also said, "These clothes suit you very well." On the way out I put my red beret on again, which brought the whole outfit together in my opinion, but Charlie again plucked it from my head and tossed it into the living room with a firm *"Non."*

Guillaume gave me an airmail envelope and a stamp so I could send my letter to Sal. Charlie and I walked all the way to the Eiffel Tower, where we joined the others. It was incredible, standing underneath it and getting a true sense of its scale. Alex, Fabrizio, and I filled each other in on our billets' apartments and neighborhoods. "There are actual prostitutes on our block!" said Fab. We couldn't help but notice that Mademoiselle Lefèvre seemed to be actively ignoring Mr. P, who stared at her with sad puppy-dog eyes.

"Uh-oh," said Alex. "I think we're witnessing ghosting in action."

Tyler stood farther back in line with his billet, Antoine. As we neared the front, he suddenly butted in front of me to stand next to Charlie. "Do something," hissed Fabrizio.

But I'd just caught sight of the elevator, which had big glass windows.

My knees started to tremble.

When it was our turn to board, I almost bolted. But Alex and Fabrizio took my elbows and guided me inside. They took me to the middle of the elevator. "Close your eyes," Alex murmured. "I'll tell you when you can open them." So I did. And I'm pretty sure I kept my whimpers to a minimum.

But when we got to the top, Kertz had the advantage. He boldly stepped right off and steered Charlie to the very edge of the viewing platform.

Everyone else got off the elevator, jostling around the boy who stood frozen in the center. "You can do it," Alex said. He and Fab held out their hands. I gripped them. They guided me out. I got closer and closer to Charlie. . . .

Then I made the mistake of looking down.

I crumpled to my knees.

Alex and Fab had to help me crawl back on all fours from the edge through throngs of annoyed tourists, and I had to sit with my head between my knees in the middle of the elevator on the way down, while above me, Tyler chatted to Charlie in French that was so much better than mine.

It was not my finest moment.

We spent the afternoon at the Louvre, which was huge and crowded. I was disappointed to see how small the *Mona Lisa* was. Most of us were still squiffy with jet lag and our feet were sore, so it was a relief when we were told we could go home.

Guillaume made us dinner again. The smells were astounding. "I am making cassoulet," he said. *"Avec une salade verte."*

Charlie spoke to him in rapid French. I caught the word *végétarien.* "But duck is not really meat," he said. "It is . . . bird."

They started to argue again in French, but I interrupted. "Please, I would like to try the duck. I promised myself I would be open to new experiences while I'm here."

Guillaume smiled triumphantly. "Good for you, Wilbur. Anyway, it is mostly white beans and tomatoes." He gave me a small portion of the cassoulet to start with. It was out of this world. I asked for seconds. Then thirds. Guillaume beamed.

"Wilbur, tell me, are you a reader?"

"Yes, sir."

"Good. That is very good. I am suspicious of people who do not read. What are some of your favorite novels?"

I was going to mention *Charlotte's Web,* as well as the Great Dune trilogy, *Lord of the Rings,* and anything by Kenneth Oppel, but suddenly I felt uncertain. Guillaume was a Famous French Intellectual; would he be dismissive of my favorites?

"I've read a number of Margaret Atwood's books and I think she's a genius," I said, which was true.

Guillaume's eyes lit up. "She *is* a genius. A Canadian treasure."

"And I read a lot of poetry. Leonard Cohen's poems in particular blow my mind."

"Ah, you are a romantic."

I probably should have stopped there, but what can I say; I wanted to impress him. So, even though I'd found the book baffling and impenetrable, I said, "Also I loved *The Stranger.* By Albert Camus."

Charlie and Guillaume both started to laugh. "Wilbur, it is pronounced *CAMOO,*" said Guillaume. "It does not rhyme with *anus.*"

I coughed. "Good to know."

"Other books?"

"Um, I also really liked *The Hunchback of Notre-Dame.*" This was a white lie, because I hadn't had time to read it before the trip, so I'd watched the animated Disney movie instead.

"Ah, it is one of my favorites, too," said Charlie.

"What did you like about this novel?" asked Guillaume.

"I liked the character of Quasimodo. He wasn't traditionally handsome, but he still wasn't afraid to sing. Oh, and I loved the talking gargoyles."

Guillaume looked at me. He looked at Charlie. He said, *"C'est un gentil garçon mais je pense qu'il est peut-être un peu simple."*

I looked to Charlie for translation. She coughed. "He says you are a very nice boy."

Later that night I lay in bed, my feet sticking out well over the end. Charlie was lying in her bed, next door. If I listened closely, I could hear her snore.

I looked out the window and I could just see a pocket of stars. For some reason, Fulton popped into my mind. I texted Sal on WhatsApp.

I am wide awake and staring at the stars outside my window in Paris. Maybe they're the same stars you will look at in a few hours. Maybe they're the same stars Fulton looked at back in the day. It's a tremendous thing to think about, isn't it? I hope you are well! Love you, Sal.

Minouche wandered in and leapt onto the bed. She kneaded her paws into the covers and purred, then she settled in on top of my stomach.

I kept staring at the stars. I had no idea what would happen during this trip, but in those moments before I fell into a deep, dreamless sleep, none of it mattered.

I was simply happy.

Paris, Days 3–4

Dear Sal,

I am writing you a second letter, but maybe I will just deliver this one by hand when I get home as it may not make it back before I do. Sorry this is rushed. Barely any time to write. Yesterday we went to the Centre Pompidou and later the science museum. I've never walked so much in my life. Today we spent the morning at Musée d'Orsay and in the afternoon we went to Mademoiselle Lefèvre's conservatoire in Saint-Germain-des-Prés to rehearse for a concert we are going to put on for the parents on our last day. Charlie and Guillaume are hosting it in their courtyard!

Charlie showed me some of her favorite paintings at the Musée d'Orsay, including one called Starry Night over the Rhône *by Vincent van Gogh. "He only sold one painting while he was alive, can you imagine? And now his paintings sell for millions." I told her I hoped I'd sell more than one poem in my lifetime, and she said she'd like to read some of my poetry! We were still gazing*

at the painting when Tyler walked up and said, "This
looks like it was painted by a toddler. I could do a better
job than that."

Charlie told him he was an idiot.

I told him he was a putz.

Later we had lunch at a falafel place in the Latin
Quarter. Tyler went to the bathroom, and when he
came back, he looked horrified. "The toilet's a hole in
the ground! What are we, in the dark ages?"

Charlie looked at me and rolled her eyes, and I did
the same.

Although I also decided that I didn't need to go that
badly, after all.

At dinner Guillaume asked how my day was and I
said, "J'ai bien joui." His eyebrows shot up, and Charlie
spit water out of her nose.

"What do you think you just said?" he asked.

"I said I enjoyed myself."

"Non. You said you have had an orgasm."

My French still needs a lot of work, Sal.

Paris, Day 5

Setbacks. We spent the morning rehearsing for our
concert again. In the afternoon we toured the Panthéon

and climbed the stairs to the viewing area at the top. Tyler pointed at the gargoyles and said it must be nice for me to be reunited with my long-lost relatives. I wanted to push him off the edge, but of course I was too scared to go anywhere near the edge.

This evening we went to a classical music concert at *L'église de la Madeleine.* I stood staring at the beautiful interior, and by the time I found Charlie, Tyler was sitting next to her. I had to sit behind them, and the seats were really close together, so I knew their legs were pressed against each other the whole time because my leg was pressed against an older French man's leg the whole time. Tyler whispered to her throughout the recital, and she whispered back, until the old man beside me leaned forward and shushed them.

She was quiet on the way home, and so was I. I didn't know what to say, or how to say it.

Later, after everyone was in bed, I tried the bidet for the first time.

It felt good, Sal. Very, very good.

J'ai bien joui.

Your BFF,
Wilbur

The definition of bravery
Isn't wielding a fist or a sword
Sometimes the definition of courage
Is simply using your words

from "Bravery" by Wilbur Nuñez-Knopf

"I LOVE YOU. YOU ARE AN INCREDIBLE PERSON. YOU ARE a winner!" I repeated my mantra over and over in the bathroom mirror the next morning, until Guillaume finally knocked on the door and told me I wasn't the only one who needed to have his morning *merde.*

We met the others in the Tuileries Gardens. Alex and Fabrizio—who were both sporting their new Parisian scarves and looking fabulous—took me aside. We stood underneath a statue by Auguste Rodin. "How's it going? Have you made any progress with Charlie?"

"I thought I was. But now, I'm not so sure. I think she might still like Tyler."

"We only have a few days left," said Alex.

"Why don't you just tell her how you feel?" asked Fab.

"Because. I might be a more confident version of myself than

I was before, but that doesn't mean I want to get knifed in the heart."

"But don't you want to *know,* one way or the other?" asked Fab.

"I'm not sure. Do I? I'm having a good time. A really good time. I don't want to blow it by suddenly making things super awkward."

We walked through the Tuileries along with the others, toward the Place de la Concorde. That's when it occurred to me that Tyler hadn't gone anywhere near Charlie all day. He was keeping to himself.

An ancient obelisk stood in the center of the Place de la Concorde, to mark the place where the guillotine had been during the French Revolution. "Thousands of heads rolled here," Charlie told me. "Including those of Louis XVI and Marie Antoinette."

I tried to block everything else out and imagine what it must have been like back then, the history, and the blood that had been spilled, right where I was standing. But it was hard to do, because a large group of tourists was standing nearby, gathered in a circle, laughing at something and taking photos. So I gave up and went to see what everyone was looking at.

It was a "pop-up" statue; it must have been placed there, stealthily, in the night. It depicted a life-sized rendition of a former U.S. president, and it was very unflattering: he was naked, with rolls of fat and wrinkles, and a saggy old-man bum. He also

had what Fabrizio called a "micropenis." Tourists were lining up to have their photos taken with the statue.

Suddenly Tyler was beside me. "Hey, Wank. Somebody made a statue of your grandpa."

I tensed up but said nothing.

"Oh, wait. He's not your grandpa. He's your best friend. You couldn't get anyone your own age to be your friend, so you got one from the Paleolithic age." He started to laugh. "He's probably just some sick old perv who likes to see young boys naked in the locker room—"

I punched him.

I wanted it to be like the movies. But I'd never thrown a punch in my life, so it wasn't like the movies at all. There was no awesome sound effect or anything like that.

"That's the best you've got?" he smirked.

I hit him again.

It still didn't have much of an impact. But now he looked mad.

He punched me back.

His punch packed a lot more wallop than mine—so much so that it knocked me to the ground. I looked up and saw, with a mixture of confusion and horror, that he was about to launch himself on top of me.

But before he could, Alex and Fab grabbed him from behind. They wrestled Tyler to the ground and sat on his chest.

Jo Lin stared, wide-eyed. Then she started to slow-clap. A moment later, almost all of the others joined in. Laura shouted, "Yes!"

Jo Lin held her hands out to me and pulled me to my feet. Charlie glared down at Tyler. "Sal Goldstein has more decency in his little finger than you have in your entire body. He is twice—no, a hundred—times the man you are! And so is Wilbur!"

And that was the scene Mr. P and Mademoiselle Lefèvre came upon when they pushed their way through the crowd.

Alex, Fabrizio, and I were sent home for the rest of the day, along with our hosts, even though they hadn't even been involved. "You represent our school. And Canada!" Mr. P shouted, his voice cracking, sweat stains forming on his shirt. "You've brought shame on our nation!" This seemed like a gross exaggeration, but we agreed that it likely had less to do with us and more to do with the fact that Mademoiselle Lefèvre was still ghosting him.

We wouldn't get to see the Musée de l'Armée. As added punishment, we weren't allowed to attend the big group dinner that night, either. Incredibly, Tyler was still allowed to go; he'd used his reptilian charms to convince Mr. P that he'd been the victim, not the perpetrator.

"He is such a jerk," Charlie fumed as the six of us walked home along the Seine—which, even as she ranted, still made me want to pinch myself—I was walking along the *Seine,* in *Paris!*— "Sometimes, the more you discover the true nature of a person, it changes how you see them. Even if they are good-looking on the outside, if you do not like their insides . . . they become sort of ugly. Do you know what I mean?"

Fab and Alex both elbowed me so hard I thought I might actually fall into the Seine.

"I take it this means you don't like him anymore?" Fab asked.

She shook her head. "Ugh, not at all. He was trying to, how do you say? Hit on me? Last night in the church. In the church! I told him I was not interested." That explained so much. His sullen behavior, even his lashing out at me. "I can't believe I ever found him attractive."

Alex and Fab had to hold back squeals of delight.

"Anyway, I am glad to be free of all the official sightseeing," said Charlie. "Allow me to show you all *my* Paris."

"We'd love to," Alex said, "but Léo and Christophe are going to take us to an outdoor flea market."

"Vintage French clothes!" added Fab.

They both murmured good luck to me before they left.

Charlie and I were on our own. It was still only eleven in the morning.

"Wilbur," she said solemnly, "I am about to make your feet very, very tired."

First, we crossed over to the Left Bank and wandered through the Latin Quarter and Saint-Germain-des-Prés, stopping at a restaurant called Les Éditeurs for a *café allongé*. We sat inside, under a big clock. The walls were lined with books, including three of Guillaume's, all in a row.

Next she took me to Ladurée, where she bought us a small, elegant box of macarons. We strolled to the Luxembourg Gardens, which was just . . . wow. The cherry blossoms were in bloom. We sat on a bench and ate the macarons, which had flavors like salted caramel and vanilla bean and pistachio—it was like biting into sweet heavenly clouds. We watched boys and girls launch wooden sailboats in the man-made pond and old men playing *boules*. It made us both think of Sal. "Next time you come, you can bring him, too," she said.

I told her I thought this was a marvelous idea.

We walked back toward the Right Bank. On the way, I bought a tea towel with French cooking phrases on it for Mup, little baguette earrings for Mum, and a notebook with a drawing of the Eiffel Tower on the cover for Sal.

On Île de la Cité, Charlie took me down a street called Quai aux Fleurs, to see a plaque. ANCIENNE HABITATION D'HÉLOÏSE ET D'ABÉLARD, 1118.

"Who were they?"

"Who were they?" she replied, astounded that I didn't know. "It is the most romantic story of all time. He was a philosophy teacher, she was his student, and they fell madly in love. They lived together in this very building and wrote beautiful love letters to each other. But her uncle was furious. He had her sent to a convent, and Abélard was castrated and became a monk."

I felt my testicles shrivel. "I bet Abélard didn't think it was romantic," I said, and she agreed that that was probably true.

We stopped for a late lunch on Île Saint-Louis, at a café called Saint Régis. I had a croque madame minus the ham, and Charlie had a croque monsieur. When we stepped back outside, she said, "Now I will show you my favorite places in Le Marais."

For the next hour or so she took me through the winding streets of her neighborhood, showing me hidden gardens and food markets. We stopped at a boulangerie; she bought an éclair, and I bought a financier. We shared. She belched when she was done.

"Last but not least, I will take you to my favorite museum in Paris," she said. "Musée de la Chasse et de la Nature."

The museum was housed in a beautiful old apartment in Le Marais, and it was easily the weirdest museum I've ever visited: part creepy, part fantastical, part inexplicable. Some rooms were filled with taxidermied animals and trophy heads (the creepy part), including a talking albino warthog. Other rooms were dedicated to certain animals—the wolf, the horse—one small room was dedicated to the unicorn. "I love it because it is like a fairy tale," said Charlie. "There is darkness, but also magic and light. When I was a child, I would spend hours in here." She showed me her favorite things, like a teddy bear floating in formaldehyde and a ceiling covered with owls' faces, peering down at us.

In a room dedicated to wolves, a drawer contained wolf poop. Actual hardened wolf poop. "There is a lot of poop in this museum," Charlie said. Then she took my hand. "And now I must show you my favorite thing of all." Her skin felt soft and warm as she guided me to an archway between two rooms. She knelt down and indicated for me to do the same. "A trompe l'oeil," she said.

There, on the baseboard, was a perfect drawing of a little mouse, peering out of its hole. It looked real. It looked three-dimensional. "It is the museum's little secret," she told me. "Very few people know it is here." Our foreheads were almost touching. She gently put a finger to my lips. "Now it is your secret, too."

Finally, exhausted, we headed home. I played head games with myself the whole way back. *Should I tell her how I feel? Should I keep my mouth shut?*

As we stepped off the elevator, I made my decision. It was now or never. I had to take the plunge.

"Charlie. I—"

The door to the apartment flung open.

Guillaume had been waiting for us. His hair looked wild, like he'd been pulling on it. *"Enfin! Tu n'as répondu à aucun de mes messages."*

"Is something wrong?"

"Margaux is in town," Guillaume said, his eyes trained on Charlie. "With Frédéric. She called me last week and I forgot to tell you. They expect to have dinner with you tonight."

The color drained from Charlie's face. *"Mais non . . ."*

"Who is Margaux?" I asked.

"My ex-wife," said Guillaume.

"My mother," said Charlie.

Charlie and Guillaume spoke in rapid-fire French. I didn't understand the words, but I understood the sentiment: Charlie didn't want to have dinner with her mom, and Guillaume was telling her she had to.

"If it would make things easier, I could go with you," I said.

Charlie looked at me. "You would do that? You would come, too?"

"Of course."

She thought about it for a moment. "All right. Then I will go." She marched ahead of us into the apartment.

Guillaume's stern expression melted, and he gave me a grateful smile. "Wilbur, that was a kind gesture." He patted my arm. "It almost makes up for pissing in our bidet."

We were supposed to meet Margaux and Frédéric at eight o'clock at a bistro in Le Marais called Le Carreau. I'd changed into a full Sal suit for the occasion.

We arrived at five after and were shown to our table in the corner. "They aren't here yet. It is typical," said Charlie. She immediately ordered us a carafe of red wine.

"But you're only fifteen," I said.

"So? Here we are not so uptight about such things. Teenagers are sometimes given wine at supper." She poured us each a glass. I felt very sophisticated. I raised mine, swirled it around, sniffed it—just like I'd seen people do in restaurants and on TV. I had a sip and tried not to make a face. It tasted sour. But Charlie had already downed hers and was pouring herself another.

At eight twenty there was still no sign of her mother. "We will give her ten more minutes, then we will leave," she declared. "We will go somewhere and have our own dinner."

I secretly wished her mother would not show.

But nine minutes later a very stylish woman—even by French standards, which is saying something—entered. She wore a gray wool dress and very high heels and a white cashmere wrap. I could smell her perfume before she reached the table. She was beautiful like her daughter, but in a more generic way. She looked like she'd had plastic surgery; the skin was pulled back around her eyes and mouth, and her expression stayed the same all evening, like she was mildly startled.

Charlie and I stood. I watched as they did three cheek-kisses: right, left, right. She gave me a look that somehow managed to be inquisitive and dismissive at once. *"Qui est-ce?"*

Charlie explained who I was in French. Margaux's cool gaze relaxed into a smile. *"Bienvenue,* Wilbur," she said, giving me the same three cheek-kisses.

A much younger man in a suit approached the table. I thought he was our waiter until Margaux said, *"Tu as trouvé où te garer?"*

He nodded. *"Oui."*

"This is Frédéric," she said. "My lover."

"*Maman!*" groaned Charlie. We had to do the same three cheek-kisses with Frédéric; honestly, with rituals like these, it's a miracle the French get anything done.

When we were all seated, Margaux scrutinized Charlie's outfit; she was in the same smock-like blouse and tights that she'd worn all day. "Is this how my daughter has been dressing? Wilbur, let me apologize on her behalf; I send her beautiful things, but she refuses to wear them."

"They are not my style, which I have tried to tell you before," said Charlie. Her voice sounded different, childlike.

"I love the way your daughter dresses," I said to Margaux. "Her unique style was one of the first things I noticed about her."

Charlie gave me a grateful look.

Margaux pursed her lips and turned her scrutinizing gaze onto me for an uncomfortably long time. "*Il a une drôle de tête. Ni beau, ni laid. Vous couchez ensemble?*"

I understood *vous couchez ensemble* because the Mumps and I had sung "Lady Marmalade" many times on our karaoke machine, and it included the lyric "*Voulez-vous coucher avec moi ce soir.*" I could feel my face get hot.

"*Maman, t'es impossible!*" Charlie said, and that set off a barrage of heated French between them.

I turned to talk to Frédéric, who sat beside me, but he was busy with his phone. I peered at the screen; it was a game of *Candy Crush.*

Eventually Charlie slumped back into her seat and crossed her arms over her chest, looking glum. Margaux asked me some questions about Canada. I asked about her life in the South of France. "It is good. I run a small clothing boutique, close to Nice." Then, to Charlie: "Shoulders back, darling."

"And you, Frédéric?" I asked politely, even though his nose was still buried in his phone. Frédéric opened his mouth to respond but Margaux beat him to it. "He is a kept man!" She laughed, and Frédéric laughed with her.

"*Oui! C'est vrai,*" he said.

Our server brought a basket of bread to the table. Charlie reached for a piece. Just before her fingers curled around it, her mother said, "You look a little heavier than you did last time I saw you, Charlotte." Charlie pulled her hand away.

I was shocked. The Mumps had never, ever made me feel bad about my appearance or my weight.

Silence descended on the table. Charlie looked like she might burst into tears.

Impulsively, I reached over and took two pieces of bread. I slathered them both with butter. Then I handed one to Charlie. I looked her in the eye and stuffed the entire piece of bread into my mouth. She did the same. I buttered two more pieces of bread, and we did it again.

Margaux huffed her disapproval.

When our server returned, Margaux ordered a bottle of wine for the table—our original carafe was long gone—and a *salade de chèvre* for her main course. Frédéric ordered the same. Charlie ordered a galette with ham, cheese, and egg.

"Charlotte, you are being ridiculous, that is too heavy."

"I will have the galette, too," I blurted. "Minus the ham. And would you share a couple of starters with me, Charlie?"

She smiled. *"Oui."* I let her choose; she ordered the escargots and a creamy mushroom tart.

Then Frédéric changed his order to the steak frites, which earned him a death glare from Margaux. *"Quoi?"* he said, before he returned to his game of *Candy Crush*.

After our server left, Margaux turned to me. "You think I am being cruel. But you must understand that Charlotte was a very chubby child."

"So was I," I told her. "But my mothers never body-shamed me."

She bristled. "I am not *body-shaming,* what a ridiculous, North American expression. I am a realist, I know how cruel people can be, and I only want the best for my daughter—"

"Which is why she abandoned me for her lover when I was seven," said Charlie in a rather loud voice.

They broke into heated French again. The server returned with the wine and poured some for all of us; Charlie drank hers quickly, grabbed the bottle, and refilled her glass.

Their arguing continued throughout our appetizers. I forced myself to eat a snail, trying not to think of the slugs that crawled through our garden. I failed on that front, and let Charlie eat the rest of them. But the mushroom tart was heaven. So was the galette.

When the waiter asked if we'd like dessert, Margaux said a firm, *"Non, merci,"* but Charlie and I said in unison, *"Oui!"*

We stuffed our faces with the most delicious dessert I've ever tasted, called *îles flottantes.*

Margaux looked into the middle distance, stone-faced.

When we left the restaurant, we had to do the kisses all over again. It took forever. The moment we were done, Margaux and Frédéric headed off toward their hotel without a backward glance.

I thought Charlie would be upset. If my Mumps had ever walked away angry like that, I'd be crushed. We had a rule that, even if we were really mad at each other, we always had to say "I love you" before we stormed out, in case one of us got hit by a bus.

But she wasn't upset. In fact, she started to laugh. As we headed down the sidewalk, she grabbed my hand. "Wilbur, you were so wonderful! I normally leave these dinners in tears. But tonight, I feel like I am floating on a cloud!"

"I suspect that's partly due to all the wine you drank." She was weaving a bit and slurring her words.

"She is so very good at making me feel so very bad. Thank you for being my knight in shining armor. You were very brave."

I had to help her get her key in the front door, because she kept missing the lock. We entered the apartment; it was dark and quiet. Guillaume had gone to bed. She turned on a small lamp in the living room and stared at me intently. "What's wrong?" I asked.

"You are the same, and yet so different, Wilbur . . . what happened?"

"I—well—a lot of things, I guess. But mostly—friends. Friends happened."

"You have changed. On the outside, yes, but on the inside too. The insides were always beautiful, but you have become stronger. More self-assured. These are very sexy qualities."

Sexy.

She had just called me *sexy*.

We gazed into each other's eyes.

This was it.

This was going to happen.

I was about to kiss the girl of my dreams in the city of love.

She leaned in. I leaned in. Our lips brushed—

"Braaaaaap!" She belched loudly, and I caught a violent whiff of ham, wine, and snails. "Oh!" she exclaimed.

She covered her mouth. Her expression went from amusement to alarm. "Oh . . ."

She bolted to the washroom.

And barfed loudly and prolifically.

I had no idea what to do. I stood outside the door and whispered, "Charlie? Are you okay?"

A few minutes later, she stepped out and stumbled to her room. I followed her in. She collapsed onto her bed. "Charlie? Is there anything I can do?"

My question was met with a groan, then silence.

"Charlie?"

She didn't answer.

She'd passed out.

I gazed down at her, lying on her bed, helpless, dead to the world.

And I did what any teenage boy would do.

I took off her shoes and placed them on the floor.

I rolled her onto her side, just to be safe.

I poured her a big glass of water and put it on her bedside table.

I put a garbage pail on the floor beside her head.

I covered her with a blanket.

Then I tiptoed out, leaving her door open in case she needed help in the night.

Throwing caution to the wind
A high-wire act without a net
Sometimes you have to take a chance
And win—or lose—the bet

From "Win, Lose, or Draw"
by Wilbur Nuñez-Knopf

"NOOOOOOO," FABRIZIO SAID THE NEXT DAY. "SUCH A drag."

"But you did the right thing," said Alex.

"Without a doubt."

"Yeah, I know." I was bleary-eyed from lack of sleep; I'd tossed and turned all night, thinking about what might have been.

We were wandering through the Palace of Versailles. It was big and overwhelming and opulent, and I realized with a pang of guilt that I wasn't really into it. For one thing, Charlie hadn't come with us. Guillaume had heard her barfing again in the night, and over breakfast she had to tell him what had happened. Her eyes and face were puffy, and she looked like she was still hurting; not once did she meet my eye.

Guillaume had been stern, but not unkind. He'd told her to go back to bed. "But I expect you to help me set up for the

236

concert in the courtyard later this afternoon." She nodded her agreement, then stumbled back to her room without a word or a glance in my direction.

"Do you think she remembers what happened?" asked Fab.

"I don't know. I'm guessing not."

We went outside and perched on the edge of a fountain. It was a hot day even though it was only early spring.

"We leave tomorrow," said Alex.

"I know."

"And the concert's tonight."

"Yeah."

"I hate to say it, Wilbur," said Fab. "But your window of opportunity may officially have closed."

"Unless," I began. An idea had started to form in the middle of the night, when I couldn't sleep, but until now I didn't dare say it out loud.

They both looked at me. "Unless?"

I told them my plan. Fab clapped, delighted. "But I can't do it alone," I said.

"I'm game if you're game," Alex said. "Although I'm also terrified." He started to blink rapidly.

"I could join in to help calm your nerves," said Fab. "I'm not scared."

"Of course *you* aren't," I said. "What would you do?"

He shrugged. "I'll think of something. I'm told I have mad go-go dancing skills."

Alex and I did our secret handshake. We taught Fab how to

do it too, which meant it wasn't quite so secret anymore, but I didn't mind.

"I'm proud of you, Wil. This is a bold move," said Alex.

"I keep asking myself: What have I got to lose?"

"Aside from any last remaining shreds of your dignity?" said Fab. "Absolutely nothing."

Then Alex started laughing, and as usual it was contagious, and pretty soon, we were all busting a gut.

It was almost five o'clock when we returned to the city. The courtyard was in the midst of being transformed. Guillaume, Charlie, and Madame Da Silva had strung up fairy lights and put out tables with actual tablecloths. I helped them set up rows of chairs.

When I'd finished with the last row, Charlie pulled me aside. "Wilbur. I am so embarrassed. I am so sorry for last night."

"It's okay, Charlie. Really—"

Guillaume interrupted. "Charlie, it is time for you to pick up the petits fours."

"*Oui, Papa.*" She left, giving him a chastened look.

I tried to interpret what she'd said to me. Was she embarrassed that she'd gotten drunk? Embarrassed that she'd barfed? Embarrassed that she'd almost kissed me? Or a combination of all three?

I had no idea.

* * *

I went upstairs and changed into one of Sal's suits. When I came back down, it was twilight, and the courtyard looked beautiful. The fairy lights twinkled. Students and parents filled the space, chatting and eating hors d'oeuvres. Everyone looked happy, except for Mr. P. He stood in a corner, looking mournfully at Mademoiselle Lefèvre, who was in a tête-a-tête with a man I hadn't seen before.

I brought Mr. P a glass of wine. "Why, thank you," he said.

"Who's the guy?"

"Geneviève's new beau, apparently."

"I'm really sorry, sir. And might I say, it was totally unclassy of her to bring him here tonight."

"That's kind of you, Wilbur. I rather thought the same myself." He had a sip of his wine.

"Thank you for arranging this trip. It's been the experience of a lifetime."

"It has, hasn't it? This was my first time in Paris, too. A dream come true . . . in spite of certain . . . unforeseen circumstances."

It was time for the concert to begin. I could hardly focus, knowing what I was about to do. The French students played first and closed out with a great rendition of "Big Yellow Taxi" by Joni Mitchell. Then the Trudeau-Manias played, and we closed out with a medley from the musical *Grease*.

Before people could start drifting away, Fabrizio clinked a glass with a fork to get everyone's attention. "Ladies and gentlemen, *mesdames et messieurs*, we have one last song to play for you tonight. A special number, with lyrics by our very own Wilbur Nuñez-Knopf, and music by Alex Shirazi."

Charlie stood by the food table, stuffing two petits fours into her mouth at once. I met her gaze.

Alex played the opening chords. Fabrizio kept his promise to take part; he grabbed my tambourine and shook it, and his body, to the beat.

My heart was pounding. My mouth was dry. But I forced it open.

And I started to sing.

Charlotte's Web

The first time I laid eyes on you
I heard angels sing a hymn
You bit me with your heavenly venom
Paralyzed my limbs
You drew me in, you held me tight
You had me in your spell
Your voice, your style, your laugh, your smile
Your voracious appetite as well

Charlotte, my own spider
You have gotten in my head

Charlotte, my own spider
You have caught me in your web

You are beautiful, dear Charlotte
You captivate me with your grin
I am stuck in the invisible silk
That you've wound around my skin
O that you would love me back
That you would feel the way I did
Until that day I remain trapped
By you, my sweet arachnid

Charlotte, my own spider
You have gotten in my head
Charlotte, my own spider
You have caught me in your web

There was complete silence when we were done. The combination of the fairy lights and the now-dark sky made it hard to see people's reactions.

People started to clap, but I could tell from the tepid nature of the applause that they were just being polite. I saw Guillaume, who was gazing at me with an inscrutable look on his face.

Someone started to laugh, and of course I recognized who it was immediately. As my eyes adjusted, I also realized he was holding up his phone. He'd recorded the whole thing. "You sounded like a cat being strangled, Wank!"

"Shut up, Tyler," someone said. Jo Lin.

"And his name is *Wilbur,* you jackass." That was Laura. I wanted to hug them both.

People started to disperse, heading back to the buffet table for more food and wine. I wound my way through the crowd, looking for Charlie. Guillaume grabbed my arm. "That was either very inspired, Wilbur, or very stupid."

"I tend to agree, Guillaume."

"Charlie is a wonderful young woman, as you are already aware. But she knows her own mind. So all I can say to you is . . . *bonne chance.*"

I finally found Charlie upstairs in the apartment. She was curled up on the couch with Minouche.

"Charlie—" I began.

"I do not like being the center of attention, Wilbur," she said.

"I'm sorry. I didn't mean to embarrass you—"

"No. It was very thoughtful. But I think we should talk."

"Okay." I sat beside her on the couch.

"I can't believe you wrote a song for me," she said. "It was very sweet. And honestly also very embarrassing."

"I didn't mean to—"

"No, no. Do not apologize. You and Alex have some talent." She took my hands in hers. "And I want you to know, I like you, too. You are one of the most wonderful men I have ever met."

"Why do I feel a *but* coming?"

"But . . . I do not think my feelings for you are as strong as your feelings for me."

There it was.

"This week I have been thinking how much I would enjoy, you know—fooling around with you—"

"Really—?"

"But I cannot do it, Wilbur. Because you are the best boy *friend* I have ever had. And I do not want to risk ruining that for one night of fun."

My mind was on fire. "I would like to suggest that we could have both? A night of fun, plus friends for life?"

"It rarely works out that way." She squeezed my hand. "I love you, Wilbur. But I don't *love* you. You understand?"

A big, fat tear of disappointment escaped my eyeball and rolled down my cheek. She wiped it away with a fingertip.

Then she leaned in and kissed me.

It was long. Lingering. It lasted until Guillaume came in a few moments later.

Even as my heart felt like it was shattering, it was magnificent.

12:01 a.m.

Sal? How are you? Are you back home? So much to tell you.

1:15 a.m.

Sal?

2:40 a.m.

Sal?

5:05 a.m.

Sal?

Guillaume woke me at five thirty a.m. to take me to the airport. He made me one last delicious café au lait. I ate one last croissant with Normandy butter. I picked up Minouche and kissed her head. I tried to keep my senses on full alert: the creamy taste of the coffee, the flakiness of the croissant, the sweetness of the butter, the scratches from Minouche's paws on the hardwood floors, the smile on the ceiling cherub's face.

Charlie's bedroom door stayed closed.

"Time to go," said Guillaume at six a.m. sharp.

As we wheeled my suitcase across the floor, her door flung open. "Why did you not wake me? Just let me brush my teeth. I am coming too!"

Guillaume drove us to Charles de Gaulle Airport in his Renault. I squeezed into the front and Charlie squeezed into the back, still in her pajamas.

We arrived just as the sun was starting to peek over the horizon. Guillaume got my suitcase from the trunk. "It has been a pleasure hosting you, Wilbur," he said. *"Tu n'es pas une lumière, mais tu es un très gentil garçon."* He embraced me, and we did the cheek-kisses. "You are welcome any time."

"Merci, Guillaume."

He climbed back into the car.

I was going to miss the Famous French Intellectual.

Charlie and I looked at each other. "Please give my love to your mothers, and to Sal," she said.

"I will."

"And please, can we Skype or WhatsApp when you are back?"

"Of course."

"I am going to miss you a tremendous amount, Wilbur. *T'es trop génial.*"

A Peugeot pulled up in front of the Renault. Tyler climbed out of the back seat.

"Wilbur?" said Charlie.

"Yes?"

"I am now going to give you your parting gift." She took my face in her hands and she kissed me. For a long, long time.

I peered out of the corner of my eye, and saw Tyler, watching us.

I'm not one to gloat, but— Oh, who am I kidding?

I gloated.

Alex and Fabrizio wanted to know everything, in play-by-play detail. So as we waited for our plane to board, I told them.

Fab actually got teary-eyed. "That's so sad, Wilbur. And yet, call me crazy, it's also kind of beautiful. A beautiful tragedy."

"I predict a *lot* of new poetry," said Alex. They took turns giving me big hugs.

"The thing is . . . I'm super sad, but I'm also super happy. It was an amazing trip."

"So, you *ne regrettes rien*?" asked Fab.

"No. If it weren't for Sal, and for you two . . . I would have stayed home. Can you imagine? If I'd missed all this?" I shook my head. "I can't wait to see Sal. I can't wait to thank him and tell him everything that's happened."

But the moment I saw the Mumps waiting for me at the Toronto airport, I knew.

I was never going to have the chance to tell Sal everything, because Sal was no longer here to tell.

Mup drove us home. I held Templeton in my arms. No lie, he put his front paws around my neck and kept them there, his own little dog hug, like he was afraid that if he let go, I'd leave again.

Mum sat in the back seat with us and told me what had happened. "He died two days ago. He had a massive stroke in the hospital. There was nothing anyone could do."

"Why didn't you call me?"

"Because it would have served no purpose, Wil, except to ruin the rest of your trip."

Part of me felt a bit angry with them. But a bigger part of me could see their logic.

"He received your letter," Mup told me. "I brought it to him at the hospital. It made him so very happy, Wil, it really did. He must have read it through three times."

We didn't say much more on the drive home. I didn't cry. I just stared out the window while Templeton licked my face.

When we arrived outside our house, everything looked so . . . normal. Sal's place looked exactly the same. I still expected him to come out onto his porch to welcome me back.

Mum made tea. A leather bag sat on the kitchen table; I recognized it as Sal's. "What's it doing here?"

"The hospital staff packed up his things. And he has no immediate family, so . . . I haven't been able to bring myself to look through it yet."

I took it into the living room. It was all of the things that Alex, Fabrizio, and I had brought him: his sweater, his slippers, the photo of Irma, his fedora, his copy of *The Amazing Adventures of Kavalier and Clay* and mine of *Charlotte's Web*.

Scrunched into the bottom of the bag was a sealed envelope with Sal's spidery handwriting on the front.

Wilbur.

I tucked Templeton under my arm and went upstairs to my room. I lay down on my bed. I tore open the letter.

Dear Wilbur,

If you are reading this, I guess it means I have well and truly kicked the bucket. You'll no doubt be feeling sad. But if you think you're sad, imagine how I feel. (Hahahaha, that was a joke!)

Since my recent brush with death (and also since I'm bored out of my nut in the hospital and Ruth Gimbel is driving me 'round the bend), I have decided I should use some of my time here wisely and write you a letter that you can only open once I've shuffled off this mortal coil.

Wilbur, when Irma passed away, I wanted to die, too. That is the truth. I couldn't imagine my life without her. I started thinking of ways to plan my exit.

Then you and your mothers moved in next door. I gave you a couple of old books about dinosaurs one day and after that I couldn't get rid of you. You kept hanging around like a bad smell. You'd just unilaterally decided we were friends. I didn't want a friend, Wilbur. I wanted to be left alone to wallow in my sorrow.

But you were tenacious, or oblivious, or both. You just kept showing up and ringing my doorbell, day after day, and I didn't have the heart to send you away. After a while, you broke me down. And do you know why? Because I came to realize that I looked forward to the time I spent with you. You were a ray of sunshine in my gloomy days. A slightly odd, but entirely sweet, young boy.

You brought me back to life, Wilbur, not once, but twice. You just didn't know about it the first time.

So when I'm gone, try not to be sad for too, too long. Know that my life has been good. Some of it has been hard. I saw the worst of humanity when I was still very young. But I also saw the best. I believe that most of my life has been beautiful. My little life is a blip in the history of our world—but it's also been a marvel. Just go lie down under Fulton again if you don't believe me.

If I can offer any advice to carry with you through your own brief time on this planet, it's this: Be kind. Be strong. Be yourself. Because "yourself," Wilbur, is a very fine human being. Even before Alex, Fabrizio, and I helped you to believe it, you were already terrific.

Radiant.

Some pig.

I consider it one of the highlights of my life to have known you.

To quote our favorite spider: "You have been my friend, Wilbur. And that in itself is a tremendous thing."

SUMMER

"THANK YOU, WILBUR. YOU'VE MADE DARRYL LOOK VERY handsome." Ms. Norrie nuzzled her face into Darryl's freshly washed and groomed fur. "Isn't that right, little munchkin? Aren't you a good-looking fellow?"

Darryl, a labradoodle, was my tenth customer at It's a Dog's Life. I'd applied for the job in June, and Robin, the owner, hired me on the spot after a Great Dane puked up two socks and a pair of men's underpants in the middle of my interview. I'd cleaned it up for her without batting an eye. Robin says I'm the best employee she's ever had. "Nothing fazes you," she says. By *nothing* I am pretty sure she means barf and poo. But I'm okay with that. I like my job. And it helps me keep my mind off Sal.

So many people came to his celebration of life! I knew he had friends, but I had no idea how many. He was popular at his synagogue, as well as with all the people he'd met through pinochle and bowling. All of the people who'd worked for him at his furniture store back in the day showed up. Lloyd, Viktor, Brenda, and a few other people from the Market were there. José came. Leah and Alice and Ethel—all the women from aquacise, really—came, too. Ruth acted like a grieving widow, which the Mumps and I privately agreed was a bit much.

The Mumps put the entire event together. They insisted that Alex and I perform a couple of songs, because they said Sal would have wanted it. We played one original ("Charlotte's Web") and one classic ("You're My Best Friend" by Queen, which we kind of mangled but nobody seemed to mind it). Fab borrowed my tambourine again, and I have to say, just like he did in Paris, he added a bit of panache. When we were done, Ethel's son asked if we'd consider playing a few songs at his daughter's bat mitzvah, before the main band takes the stage, and we said yes. We have a month left to work on our numbers, which is a relief.

Charlie insisted that we livestream Sal's celebration of life so she could watch it from her apartment in Paris. She and I FaceTime regularly, about once a week. I still kind of love her, if I'm honest. But I also love being her friend. We talk about everything: about Sal, about my new job, about the play she's in this summer, which is a French, all-female version of *Twelve Angry Men* (called, naturally, *Twelve Angry Women*). Sometimes we just read. There's something comforting about looking up from my book and seeing her on my computer screen.

I miss Sal every day. I still have moments when I forget he's gone, and I'll go to knock on the wall, or I'll think of a story I have to tell him. Then I'll remember, and I'll just have to go somewhere for a private cry.

I wish I could tell Sal that he was right. I didn't get the girl, but the trip to Paris was still the best ten days of my life. I wish I could tell him thanks. Not just for that, but for bringing Alex back into my life, and, yes, for bringing Fabrizio into my life, too.

Because of Sal, my trip to Paris is my new Defining Moment.

I no longer let myself be defined by what happened in seventh grade.

And I definitely don't let myself be defined by Tyler Kertz.

When we got back from Paris, he tried to humiliate me all over again by posting his video of "Charlotte's Web" on YouTube. Everyone from my school watched it, and I guess they told friends to watch it, because it wound up getting quite a few views. Nothing near viral, but close to a thousand.

At first I thought it was going to be like my seventh grade time capsule letter all over again. It got quite a few nasty comments, of the "Worst voice ever!" and "Sounds like a hyena in heat!" variety.

But the crazy thing is, most people at my school—especially the girls—had a different point of view. Once, when Tyler started imitating my voice and lyrics in the hall, Poppy said, "Shut up, Tyler. You wish you had half of Wilbur's talent."

"Yeah," said Olivia the oboist. "It was *so* romantic."

His attempt to make me feel like crap mostly backfired. He still called me Wank for the rest of the school year, but more and more people started calling me Wilbur again. It's finally getting old. *Tyler* is getting old. And it's not just me who feels that way. Jo Lin, Oliver, Laura, Alex, Fabrizio, and all the others who'd quietly borne his insults—I think we all woke up and realized he's just one guy. He's lost his power to make us feel like trash. Once, after one of our final band practices in June, he started ribbing me—and I just looked right over his head, stepped around him, and kept on walking. After everything that's happened, I no longer care about Tyler Kertz.

He is the zero.

The Mumps have really been there for me these past few months, without being too over-the-top. We talk a lot, and cry a lot, but we also laugh a lot, sharing memories of our great friend and neighbor. I still go to aquacise with Mup; I didn't want to, but Mup told me the ladies would be heartbroken if I didn't. "They can't lose you both at the same time." It was a fair point.

So I go. It isn't easy, especially before and after in the change room where Sal and I had so many conversations, but I can see it really does bring the ladies some comfort, and I think it's what Sal would have wanted.

And get this, Mum has managed to get every last penny of my back pay from Foot Long! At first, she called Mr. Chernov incessantly, asking politely for my money. When that didn't work, she did some research and found out you have to be at least fifteen to do food prep. So she threatened to report him for using underage workers. All this time I'd been breaking the law without knowing it!

Anyway, it did the trick.

I know I shouldn't let my mum fight my battles.

But once in a while, it's pretty nice to have someone who is so firmly in your corner.

Once or twice a week, the Mumps and I go over to Sal's house to pack things up. Sometimes Alex and Fabrizio come, too. Thanks to his death cleaning, and the clear instructions he left in his will about where things should go, there isn't a lot to do. Still, I've found a few treasures that I'm keeping. Some photos of Sal when he was a young man, freshly arrived in Canada. The photo of him and Irma in Paris. His landing papers. His gray fedora.

Oh, and also.

Sal left us his house.

Yes. That's right. We were stunned when his lawyer contacted us. Sal's instructions were for us to sell it and pay off our mortgage, and that's exactly what we've done. There was a small amount of money left over, and that's gone into an education fund for me.

His house sold just a few weeks ago, to a family with two

little kids. They move in at the end of the month. The mom has already asked if I'd consider babysitting. I said I'd have to think about it. It's going to be weird at first, seeing new people living in Sal's old place.

But maybe, eventually, it will be nice, too.

I changed into my running gear and got Templeton, who was dozing on a doggy bed in the front room of It's a Dog's Life. It's the other great perk of this job; Robin doesn't mind if I bring him to work. I put on his leash and shouted toward the back. "Bye, Robin, see you tomorrow."

"Bye, hon! Have a good Friday night!"

Templeton and I jogged home.

I was looking forward to my evening. Alex, Fab, and I were going to get together and go for a swim at Sunnyside pool, then we were going back to Alex's. He was going to cook a full Persian feast for us, and then we were going to try for the umpteenth time to teach Fab how to play Carcassonne. The three of us spend a lot of time together. They check in on me all the time and invite me to hang out with them more than they need to. Sometimes I feel like a third wheel, so I am trying to wean myself from spending quite so much time with them—but not tonight.

When we got back to our place, I fed Templeton, then I went upstairs to have a quick shower and get changed. I wasn't meeting Alex and Fab for another couple of hours, and I could feel all of my emotions welling up, so I told the Mumps I was heading back out. "I'll be home before they arrive," I said.

As I left, they shared a concerned look.

I took the subway from Queen up to Bloor along the University line and walked the rest of the way to the ROM. I've been going there at least once a week since I got home from Paris. It helps me feel close to Sal. I go and lie down under Fulton, and José lets me stay there for as long as he can, because he misses Sal, too. I think about the things Sal told me. About how, in the history of the Earth, our lives are a blip. I sometimes swear I feel him lying beside me, saying: "Miraculous! Tremendous! But still a blip!"

It is oddly comforting.

I flashed my membership card and headed straight for Fulton. But when I got there, I saw a pair of legs sticking out from between the two metal slabs. Someone was lying in my spot. For a split second I thought it was Sal—my mind, playing a nasty trick. Then I remembered (a) he was dead, and (b) he did not have sparkly silver sandals. Or red hair.

"Mitzi?"

She gazed up at me. "Wilbur!" She was in shorts and a T-shirt. She patted the floor beside her. I lay down. "I kind of hoped I might run into you here sometime."

"You come here a lot?"

She nodded. "Ever since I ran into you that day. Sometimes I just feel kind of . . . I don't know . . . overwhelmed . . ."

"By what?"

"By life? And I remembered this sort of calmed you down, so I decided to try it, and it works! It sort of calms me down, too."

"Well. That's cool."

"Hey. I quit Foot Long."

"Yeah?"

"About a month after you left. I have a job at Meeplemart now."

"The board game store? I love that place."

"Me too. It's a way better job."

"I have a better job too, at a dog groomer's."

"That's perfect for you. Do you still run?"

"I do. Three times a week. You?"

"Yup. Hey, did you wind up going to Paris?"

"I did."

"How was it?"

"Life-changing," I said without hesitation. "How about your Pennsic Wars?"

"Just came back last week. It was mind-blowing."

We lay in silence for a while. I could see José out of my peripheral vision; he was pretending not to notice us.

"How've you been otherwise?" Mitzi asked.

I thought about how to answer that. "Not great. My best friend died."

"Seriously? Wilbur, that's terrible."

"He was eighty-five. But still."

ACKNOWLEDGMENTS

I was lucky enough to go to the UK a few years ago on a small book tour and traveled one day with a charming and unflappable twenty-something publicist, Harriet Dunlea. She told me in passing that she took aquacise for seniors once a week with her mom. Something about this image just made my heart swell, and I told her, "Careful, Harriet, I'm going to put this into a book one day." I swear it's that image that started me on the journey of discovering the friendship between Wilbur and Sal. So, people who spend time with authors, be very careful what you let slip, unless you're prepared to see it in the pages of a book.

By the time a novel is published, one hopes it looks effortless. But the process is often like pulling teeth. I owe a huge thanks to the people who took early looks at the manuscript: Susan Juby and Linda Bailey, two of our finest Canadian authors, and Göran Fernlund, one of the finest Swedish Canadian husbands. And my intrepid agent, Hilary McMahon, whose honesty, hard work, and enthusiasm are always appreciated.

My editors—Tara Walker, Wendy Lamb, and Charlie Sheppard—are a triumvirate of talent, and I'd have been lost without their thoughtful notes and encouragement. Peter Phillips, Dana Carey, and Chloe Sackur, you are all marvels, as are your entire teams.

"I'm really sorry to hear that."

"Thanks."

"My best friend died, too," she said. "Franklin."

It took me a moment.

"Not that I'm comparing the two. But my parents are separating too, and—I don't know. I feel like I can't control anything. And Franklin was just always . . . there, you know?"

Because he was in a terrarium and couldn't go anywhere else, I thought. But all I said was, "I'm really sorry, Mitzi. That's a lot to be going through."

Her fingers grazed mine. I didn't know if it was an accident, or on purpose. I could smell her hair, and it smelled good, like coconut.

Suddenly I pictured my seventh-grade time capsule letter, the last sentence I'd written: *He who takes no chances, wins nothing!*

I turned my head toward her. "Would you like to get together some time?"

"Yes. I would."

"Great. How about—"

"Tomorrow?"

"Oh. Yes. Awesome. Run? Coffee?"

"Both?"

"Deal."

Then she wrapped her hand around mine. Absolutely, definitely, not an accident.

I looked back up at Fulton. I heard Sal's voice, clear as a bell: "What a marvel life is."

Once the manuscript was at a stage where I could let other eyes see it, I got feedback from a wealth of amazing authenticity readers. I was tickled when Dr. Rob Bittner agreed to read the manuscript. Rob, your comments were invaluable.

To my friends Jennifer Daley and Melissa Likely, I'm so grateful for your considered read and your notes on the Mumps. Olly is a lucky boy to have such wonderful parents.

To my young beta readers: Ryan Brown—who, full disclosure, happens to be my awesome nephew—started the first Pride event in Owen Sound, Ontario, I am enormously proud of his accomplishments. Thank you, Ryan, for your considered feedback. Noah Poursartip also gave me fabulous notes, especially on the Alex Shirazi character. It's a toss-up who will become prime minister of Canada first: Noah or Ryan? We'll be in good hands in either case.

I also wanted a young female beta reader, but most of my friends' girls are now in their twenties. Then I realized I had the perfect person hiding in plain sight: Eden Summer Gilmore had recently been hired to play the daughter of the lead on my new TV series, *Family Law*. Eden, thank you for your considered notes. One day people will read this paragraph and think, "She got *Eden Summer Gilmore* to read her manuscript?? *The* Eden Summer Gilmore??"

This is the first time I've set a book somewhere other than Vancouver. B.V.—Before Vancouver—I spent twelve years living in Toronto. I went to post-secondary school there (Ryerson) and began my TV career there (writing for shows like *Degrassi Junior High* and *Ready or Not*). I lived all over the west end, including, for a few years, in a cockroach-infested apartment right next door to Kensington Market. Oh, how I loved it. I had so many adventures in the Market—including getting punched, not once but twice, on two separate occasions by two separate strangers (it's a long story. I was fine). So I wanted to set one book in a city I still visit regularly. Thank you to my mom, Eleanor, and my stepdad, Charles, for letting me crash at their place while I toured the city to make sure my descriptions were accurate.

This novel also wound up being my love letter to another of my favorite cities: Paris. *Merci beaucoup* to Valérie Le Plouhinec—she has translated every one of my novels into French (and will hopefully translate this one, too), and she does such a fabulous job. She read this manuscript and had invaluable feedback when I massacred the French language or got facts about a place wrong. And to Gilberte Bourget, from whom I shamelessly lifted Charlie's adamant *"Non!"*, and Sophie Giraud at Hélium for so faithfully publishing my novels, and for managing to get me invited to Paris on numerous occasions for festivals. *Paris, je t'aime!*

A couple of years ago I had a long, hard ride with my cycling club, Glotman-Simpson. Afterward we stopped for food, and mine took a long time to come. At one point the waiter brought out a chicken jalapeño burger, which no one had ordered. After he walked away, I, getting hangry, said, "I should have had the chicken jalapeño burger." One of my cycling friends scoffed, "That will be on your tombstone. Your life's biggest regret." Thanks, Matt Dwinnell, both for keeping it real, and for the inspiration behind the title of one of the self-help books within the book.

Lastly, I owe a debt to E. B. White—his famous children's novel, *Charlotte's Web*, helped me find my way toward the themes of this novel. Melissa Sweet's absolutely delightful biography of E. B., called *Some Writer!*, was also really helpful, and I highly recommend it.

ABOUT THE AUTHOR

SUSIN NIELSEN is the author of *Word Nerd, Dear George Clooney: Please Marry My Mom, The Reluctant Journal of Henry K. Larsen, We Are All Made of Molecules, Optimists Die First,* and *No Fixed Address.* She got her start writing for the original hit TV series *Degrassi Junior High,* and has written for more than twenty Canadian TV series. Her books have won critical acclaim and multiple awards both at home and around the world, including the Governor General's Literary Award and the UKLA Award, and have been translated into many languages. But best of all, a reluctant reader once told her that her books "weren't trash" and congratulated her on a job well done. Nielsen took this as high praise indeed. She lives in Vancouver with her family and two naughty cats.

susinnielsen.com